To Waltz With A White Horse
By: Ron Shepherd

**Global Video Marketing
& Graphic Design**
Publishing Division

First printing
Email: peaceriverbooks@ronshepherd.com
Website: www.ronshepherd.com

ISBN: 0-9769455-2-5
PUBLISHED BY GLOBAL VIDEO MARKETING
PUBLISHING DIVISION
www.globalvideomarketing.com
Minnesota


Printed in the United States of America

To Billy,
Lock n Load

# Table of Contents

## Prologue:

Wars have been a means of settling arguments for longer than man has been somewhat civilized. One person described war as being "Old men sending young men off to settle arguments".

Some contend that certain wars never do come up with a clear victor, mainly because the politicians have neither the backbone nor the will to go that extra mile. The soldiers are the willing pawns, moved around the globe like players in a chess game. When the politician says go here or go there, the soldier is not only willing, but he gives everything he has to his country and sometimes that means his life.

In the hills of West Virginia back in the early days of World War II, a boy, still too young to enlist, lied to his recruiter about his age and joined the Army. Young Billy Kuhn answered the call and went off to fight an enemy in Europe that he knew little of. He fought bravely for the folks back home and grew up fast and hard.

What could have possessed a young man to give up a good life in the hills and leave his friends and family behind? Is it possible that he heard the call from those politicians or maybe he just wanted to help the country he loved.

Today, we enjoy our lives in this free country and seem to be working hard at forgetting those who fought to keep us free. Each year, those same politicians cut deeply into any services for our military disabled. They are allowed to do so because there are fewer and fewer wounded left to complain. Without a popular war to champion, the Washington bureaucrats turn a deaf ear to the pleas for funding.

When Billy was so weak that he could hardly stand, he still came to attention and saluted as "Old Glory" came by on Veteran's Day.

He died not long ago in a VA hospital, fighting for the benefits that were owed him and did so with the same tenacity he fought the Germans in Europe. Sure, he got some care, but not enough to save his life.

So what is it that we actually owe our disabled veterans? We owe them our thanks.

Each time you see a polling place, thank a vet. Whenever you see our flag carried by a color guard, thank a vet. That court house downtown? Yes. Yes. Yes. Were it not for our veterans, we'd have a dictator sitting inside controlling every facet of our lives.

So when you hear of the VA asking for more money, tell Washington to lend a helping hand and thank a vet, that you aren't forced to speak Japanese or German.

## Chapter: 1    First Blood

Breathe dammit. That's right. Inhale slowly and then let it back out again. Do it again. Inhale slowly and let it back out again. I just can't do it. No matter how hard I try, there is no smooth rising and falling of my chest. It bounces around as if I'm trying to remember how it's done. All around me it's starting to look like a Keystone Cops fire drill with people running everywhere.

Not more than seventy yards away, a mortar round explodes leaving behind a young GI holding his hands over his eyes, screaming into his manmade darkness.

I try not to think about the fact that my life blood is running out onto the mud of this damned rice paddy. Panic is rising within me and it threatens to abscond with my sanity. The medic is doing his best to stop the bleeding and my squad has set up a quick defense perimeter. It seems as if people are yelling all around me. The air is heavy with the smell of rotting vegetation and it almost takes my breath away. It's the kind of smell no one gets used to.

## Ron Shepherd

There is a moment of quiet and I look off to the west. The sun is starting to set and through the haze of exploded artillery rounds the sky is a dark red.

Breathe in slowly and then let it out. I just can't seem to get it right. I feel a knot the size of a basketball growing inside my gut. I'm very scared right now, but it's nothing I can't handle. I try hard to think about my breathing. Through the haze of pain and drugs I see a man standing next to me holding an IV bag with a line that feeds into my arm. The pain is easing some, but I feel very dizzy. The morphine is starting to do its intended job. Over a few clicks to the north I can hear the sound of heavy artillery rounds hitting the soft soil of the rice paddies, but right now I just plain don't give a damn. For just a moment the taste of metal fills my mouth as if I had a piece of aluminum foil I was chewing on.

The pain makes a return trip and I look down for the source of the problem. My right leg is gone below the knee. I never felt it leave. The explosion just seemed to completely cover me with noise, extremely loud noise. A medic is wrapping gauze around my leg and my ears are ringing loudly.

I hear someone yell "incoming", and instinctively I try to turn and cover my face. The round explodes several yards away, throwing up a black cloud of mud and shrapnel. I feel a bee sting me in my shoulder. Small arms fire starts again, sounding like popcorn popping on the stove, then it quits. I can hear excited voices talking nearby. One guy is looking at a map and his buddy is calling firing coordinates into a radio.

# To Waltz With A White Horse

I feel something near my nose and reach up to see what it is. A big gob of stinking rice paddy has landed on my face.

On the other side of the opening I see two Thuds dropping napalm into the jungle. As quickly as it is released from the planes, they bank hard left and roll off in a cloud of jet fuel smoke. A cloud of deep red with black mixed in for effect, rises high above the jungle. I hope somebody brought the marshmallows.

Someone is trying to move me. I open my eyes and see that I am on a stretcher and two grunts are carrying me toward a chopper. I'm having a hard time gathering my thoughts.

They slide me inside and I hear the engine of the great Pegasus take a deep breath and come to life, lifting me from the earth to the sky. Three nice neat holes appear in the side of the chopper right beside my head, likely from some VC sniper. I close my eyes and try hard to remember home. Next to me, a GI on a stretcher is waving his arms wildly.

The rotor blades bite hard into the hot and humid air, shaking the aircraft violently with each rotation. The fighting's over for me now. No one legged grunts in this war.

I can feel someone touch my hand and it's the medic once again checking for a pulse. It doesn't matter to him right now if it's strong or weak, but it's just gotta be there. Breathe. Inhale slowly and then let it back out again. He bends down and yells in my ear.

"How ya doin'?"

The words register in my mind, but it doesn't seem that a

response is required. He has large black eyes and they flash like lightning in the frame of his dark brown face. He looks so damned alive.

"Ya need more junk?" he yells.

Still, the words come in, but I just can't seem to put together any kind of a response. I can feel my toes tingling and it seems to awaken me. My thoughts for a short time are sharper and I realize that those toes are probably miles from me right now. I close my eyes tightly and the stench and the sounds of Viet Nam disappear ever so slowly, replaced by the smell of the big pine trees on the north side of Hale Lake.

My pal Rusty and I have gotten hold of a nice sharp single bladed ax and planned on building a cabin in the woods. We sized up a likely candidate for our first effort and went at it in a most serious manner. I chopped until my arms got sore and then Rusty took his turn at it. We continued taking turns back and forth for the better part of two hours. The boy scout ax really wasn't doing much damage to the great pine tree so when the sun started to set, we left the woods and headed home for some supper. The great tree had withstood the efforts of two would be cabin builders.

The next morning as I sat on the back steps of the house watching the dew sparkle and evaporate in the summer sun, Rusty came once more to see if I wanted to continue building "the cabin". I grabbed the ax and we headed down the road to the big stand of pines. It was early in the morning and our energy level was high. I took the first turn at chopping and

must have went at least a half of an inch into the great pine
when I tuckered out. Rusty, full of energy as a nine year old
can be, commenced to chopping again. His efforts gave up
some small chips, but nothing that would cause the giant to
weaken and fall.

Near noon, we decided to go back home and have
something to eat. Our efforts so far hadn't caused much
damage to the big tree. We figured that if we kept at it, we
could move in by Sunday morning and spend the entire fall and
winter in our new home.

The next morning we headed back to the big pine tree near
Hale Lake. This time we put our heads together trying to figure
where the giant would fall. Actually it didn't seem to matter
much just as long as we got it down where we could work on
it some. We'd cut it into twenty foot pieces and just stack them
up until the walls were as tall as we needed. Actually there
wasn't much to building a cabin. There were many such trees
near Birds Eye, our favorite winter sliding hill.

We chopped hard until nearly noon and once again headed
home for lunch. As we walked along, Rusty asked if we had
a saw at home. He figured that a saw might just save us a bit
of time. We both had listened to the old lumberjacks at the
boarding house tell of how they would saw down the great
red pines, so if we had a smaller saw, we might just be able to
handle it. I went into the garage and there hanging on the back
of the workbench was a long saw with a handle on both ends.
I climbed up on the bench and took it down from its perch,

handing it to Rusty. Dad wouldn't mind if I brought it back when we were done, but I guess I probably should have asked.

After a hurried lunch, we took the big saw and went back up into the pines. Somehow it felt different this time. It was more like being lumberjacks and heading off to work. The big pine was still there just as we had left it. The tree was nearly two feet across and the notch we had made in two days of chopping was only about five inches deep. We held the saw up to the tree and started to pull back and forth as a steady stream of sawdust fell to the ground. After a short while, we stopped and measured our progress. We had gained a couple more inches.

The sun was starting to set and we headed back home once again for some supper. As we walked in the near darkness Rusty said that it sure would be nice when we didn't have to walk back and forth all the time and could just stay at "the cabin". I figured that maybe we wouldn't even have to go to school any more either since we'd have a place of our own. The prospects of this new life gave us renewed strength for the next day.

The plan was set and the next morning we each had a sandwich and a bottle of coke, enough supplies for the entire day. We walked across the dew wet grass in the early morning and took the saw from its place in the garage. As we walked along toward the big pines, I envisioned a new home with a fireplace and a large supply of hot dogs and marshmallows.

The tree was still there just as we had left it, but there was now getting to be a much deeper cut. I slipped a small piece of paper into it and figured that we were nearly half way through. We put the saw in once more and started pulling back and forth on it. The day was beautiful and it warmed up fast with bright puffy clouds moving by in the sunshine. After a couple hours, the wind started to come up some. We were both sweating from exertion and then it happened. The great pine gave out a loud cracking sound and we froze in our tracks looking at each other. Nothing further happened so we started to saw once more. There it was again, a loud crack. Then the wind came up for just a moment and the tree started to move.

Rusty gave out the long awaited signal. "Timber" he yelled and we stood back to see the giant fall. It moved ever so slowly toward the lake and then a gust of wind pushed it back the other direction and it stopped cold, with the precious two man saw held tightly in its grip. Nothing happened for a long time, so once more we advanced upon our victim. We grabbed the saw and found to our dismay that it was held fast by many tons of red pine. There was no way we could get the saw out and near noon decided to go home. Our place in the woods, "the cabin", would have to remain unfinished.

Later in the fall, Dad asked if I had seen the saw. Being a terrible liar, I had to confess that I was the one who had taken it and told Dad about how we were going to build a cabin. I took him out to the big stand of red pine and there, right where I had left it, was the saw. It was sitting on a large red pine stump and the great tree we worked so hard on was lying on the ground. The wind had, at some time in the last few weeks, changed direction, blowing it over.

"Now, whatcha gonna do with it?" asked Dad.

I wasn't a bit sure, but that was indeed a big tree. Dad stepped it off, and it came to just over ninety feet. He told me that it weighed many hundreds of pounds and would take large machines just to move it. Being just nine years old, I figured that maybe we just might want to wait on the cabin for a while.

The chopper changed direction and speed and I awoke for a bit. The large black eyes of the medic stared back at me. A wisp of a smile crossed his face and it gave me a small degree of confidence that things might get better. On the stretcher next to me, the blanket had been pulled up to cover the face of the prior occupant. His days of smelling this filthy place had come to an end during the flight. Earlier his arm had been flailing around as if he was trying to fly. I hope he made it.

As the chopper settled on the tarmac, the ambulance rolled up close to transfer the wounded to the triage area. On this day, there were no others waiting. The morphine was starting to wear off and great waves of pain flooded my brain, attempting to capture my consciousness. A gruff sounding doctor lifted what was left of my leg and quickly cut off the bandage, letting the blood once more start to flow. The whole place smelled like disinfectant. He gave some orders to a dark haired nurse and covered my leg with more bandages. The pain became too great and the surrounding room started to spin.

"Do you need more stuff for pain?" asked the doctor. His breath smelled worse than the rice paddy I just came from.

# To Waltz With A White Horse

I nodded my head and watched him deliver another load of dream serum into my IV line. It took just a short while to start working, and slowly, ever so slowly, I made the trip back home again, flying slowly through the clouds on the back of a morphine filled syringe.

I was going down Hale Lake in my old cedar strip boat. It had a flat bottom and one broken oar. I sat in the bow and paddled the boat backwards. The sky was a bright burning blue with small puffy clouds drifting over the lake. A pair of eagles cut giant arcs across the sky. It was hot, as hot as Minnesota gets in the summer. The sweat dripped into my eyes making it difficult to see. Over across from the pump house was a small bay where the water was always calm. An old abandoned beaver lodge sat near the shore, small trees growing from it.

I sat still in the boat watching the show under the surface. The great hunters of the lake hid near the reeds and grasses, waiting for their next meal to swim by. There were some large bass swimming around but they didn't seem to have any interest in the gob of worms I threw to them. I rowed over to shore and waded in the tall reeds looking for a frog to use for bait. A large one made a fatal jump to get away and I had my bait for that big bass. I rowed back out a short distance and then cast the frog back to where I had seen the fish. After each cast, I waited until the ripples stopped on the water and slowly pulled the frog back to me. After several casts, nothing seemed interested so I decided to head back across the lake and home for supper. I stood up in the boat and with the rod, slapped the now dead frog onto the water, tearing it loose from the hook. The ripples in the water slowed and faded, and the frog settled slowly toward the bottom.

To my amazement, a sequence of events took place that actually made me fearful of what was in the water. The frog had settled a couple feet down when a nice three pound bass rushed out and grabbed it. He just sat there with the meal in his mouth. Then, in just a small part of a second, a giant northern pike had the bass crossways in his mouth, swimming slowly back to his lair in the weeds. He was an actual giant weighing way over thirty pounds, much larger than I had ever even heard of.

The show was over, and I had been chosen to be the witness. This event was never spoken of and I kept it deep inside fearing that nobody would believe such a tale. It was quite a sight for a ten year old boy.

I was slowly paddling back across the lake and my eyes fluttered open. I was in a brightly lit room with several angels all dressed in white surrounding me. One of them was praying softly and said something about "dominoes, dominoes, who brought the dominoes". He made the sign of the cross over his chest and moved on to the next table.

"Can you hear me Sergeant?" asked one of the angels.

I couldn't make my mouth work, but my mind still seemed fairly clear.

"Go ahead and put the mask on him." said one of them.

An angel put a large rubber Halloween mask on me and all I

could think of was "trick or treat".

"Now count backwards from one hundred." she said.

"Ninety-eight, ninety-seven, ninety...."

I walked across the frosty back yard heading for Mrs. Korpi's house so I could yell trick or treat. It was Halloween and I was seven years old. I had a small paper bag to store the ill gotten gain and was a bit afraid of the dark. There had been witches dressed in black and large pumpkins with scary faces running through my mind all day.

It was cold outside, and in northern Minnesota, it was getting close to snowing. October 31$^{st}$ was the end of fall, and serious winter storms were just around the corner.

I stepped up on the porch and knocked on the door. Mrs. Korpi opened it and in a small and slightly afraid voice I announced myself with "trick or treat". She smiled and put a small piece of candy into the bag. She said that she wondered who it was under that mask. I stepped off the porch and walked toward Johnson's house, my next victim. There was a large oak tree on the way and as I walked under it, I heard an owl say "Who Ooo." Then it leaped from the branch and flew across the full moon, no doubt headed off to scare some other kid like me. A combination of fear of the dark and a vivid imagination made Halloween a time of great excitement.

Over to Firman's for one of her great cookies and then a stop at Kjarvstad's pretty much made for a full evening. As I walked in the near darkness, I saw a couple boys coming toward me and with masks on. I didn't know who they were.

I just kept walking and as I went by them, the taller one made a grab for my bag of candy. I was way to quick for him and started to run for home with them right behind me. They were so close I could hear them breathing. Then just as I got near home, they got me. A slight push from behind sent me sprawling. The tall one took the bag of goodies and the other one pulled off my mask.

"I think we better check his vitals once more." said one of them.

"How are you feeling Sergeant?"

The angel had bright blue eyes and a smile that would kill. She was all dressed in white.

"You'll be needing more pain medication in a while. I want you to just wave your hand when you need anything and I'll be able to see you."

I looked around the room and it was filled with nearly a dozen other GI's, victims of this so called war. Some were in full body casts and some had parts missing. It appeared to be a large ward, but I wasn't sure where I was or even what country I was in.

After another couple hours, I was forced to raise my hand.

"Teacher. Teacher. I need to go to the bathroom."

Another nurse came over and stuck a thermometer in my face.

"How are you feeling?"

"Ah muma hum a goo doom."

"Oh that's good." she said.

## To Waltz With A White Horse

You dumb ass, I gotta go to the bathroom. No sense
trying to talk right now. Finally she came back and took the
thermometer from my mouth. She held it up to the light and
read the good news.

"Still got a bit of a fever, but you've only been here a couple
days. It's starting to drop some. You had a visitor this morning.
Your house girl Uuan came in to see you."

That sounded to me like I might just be somewhere close to
where I started from a few days ago.

"She'll be back in a couple hours."

Once more I told her that I had to go to the bathroom.
She said that she'd bring me a bedpan. A what! A bedpan,
the most dreaded of all hospital torture devices. She grinned
at me sweetly and told me to lift my gown. My gown! Yup,
my gown. A feeling of indignation swept over me for just
a moment and then I felt resigned to use the contraption. I
wiggled and shuffled around until I was perched atop the great
stainless steel pan. There, I made it, and only about a dozen
people watched as I sat there red faced, bearing down hard.
I was totally embarrassed, but nearly all of my audience had
been in the same situation, and the ones that hadn't, still had it
to look forward to.

Later on in the afternoon, Uuan walked in with a big grin
on her face. Her eyes were as big as baseballs and everything
about her seemed to radiate happiness. She had a small basket
with her and inside was a gift. She handed me a piece of
newspaper rolled in the shape of a cone, containing a large

helping of deep fried shrimp. It was the most wonderful present I could even imagine.

One afternoon a few months back, Uuan and I had taken a walk down to the ocean. I saw an old boat partially filled with yellow flowers, sand and broken pieces of wood. I had her sit beside it and used up three rolls of film just on this one subject. She was the prettiest woman I had ever seen. Then on the way back, some kid on a scooter roared by and grabbed the camera from me, breaking the strap. The days photography however is still fresh in my mind.

Today she was dressed in a red and yellow sarong and had her hair tied back with yellow ribbons. It was a stark contrast to this drab and dreary place. We ate together, Uuan sitting cross legged on the foot of the bed. Then she pulled out a can of Miller High Life beer for me. What a gal! She'd thought of everything, everything that is except for a church key, so I saved the beer for later.

As we talked, Uuan got a most serious look on her face. She looked at my IV and then over to the large gob of bandages on my leg. Then she touched my hand and said, "Maybe you die." She smiled brightly.

While to her, this may have been the best thing since fried rice, it was nonetheless, a long way from being a comforting thought to me. To Uuan, it meant eternity sitting at the feet of her master. She was a devout Buddhist and her faith carried her through years of very difficult times. She was most certainly a good friend.

## To Waltz With A White Horse

A steady stream of wounded came and went in that little hospital ward. The whole thing stunk. Back in the world they were protesting the presidents war with marches and demonstrations. Some just took the cowards way out and instead of helping their country, fled like scared children, north to Canada. When it was nice and safe again, they'd try to sneak back into the U.S. slithering on their belly.

I had visions of my favorite TV show Wild Kingdom with Marlin Perkins and his faithful pal Jim. They would be on the trail of the giant killer snakes of Booga Booga paddling through vast herds of alligators. Marlin would spot an absolutely huge one and then with those magic words "Get him Jim!", the fight was on. Jim would dive over the side of the dugout canoe and do battle with whatever the boss told him to get. As far as I was concerned, that was also the way the Army worked. Take that hill, and by the way, don't worry about casualties. Then after a terrible battle where many good men get killed and wounded, the boss in Washington would say, "Oh hell. I was only kidding. Give 'em back their damned hill." I figured that this war would go a lot better if some of those politicians came over to help for a week or two.

Time wore on and still my fever wouldn't allow me to leave the country. They said that I had to be "normal" for 72 hours. Little did they know, but normal had been evicted many years ago. I had no idea what it even meant.

Early one morning a very pretty nurse came in and asked if I'd had enough of that needle. She gently removed it from my arm and untaped me from the board that kept it all straight. It took the better part of the day until I could finally bend my elbow again. With that out of the way, it gave me a bit more freedom to explore. In the mornings after things would settle down some, I'd be helped into the wheel chair and go on a search for some conversation.

First stop was the guy next to me in the full body cast. All that showed were his feet, his hands and his head. He was a black man and had been pretty close to losing it in the jungle. His name was John and he was from South Carolina. He seemed to be pretty quiet, but just how much hell can you raise in a full body cast.

"Hey John! How ya doin' today?"

"Been better." he mumbled.

"Ya, this whole thing is a bummer. I had an idea last night. How 'bout I write a letter home for ya?"

John's dark eyes lit up.

"Sure would appreciate that Sarge."

I rolled my chariot over to the nurse and asked for some paper and a pencil. She had a large supply along with envelopes. I thanked her and said that I'd be writing a lot for the guys that couldn't handle a pencil yet.

I wheeled back over to John and saw that his previous sparkling eyes had been replaced by an awfully long face.

"Who would you like to address this to John?"

"If you can Sarge, I need you to write two for me."

"Sure. I got nothing better to do. Who's the first one to?"

"Mr. & Mrs. Wilfred Davis, 2328 Old Mill Road, Riverton, South Carolina. Got it?"

"Yup. Go ahead John, but don't go too fast."

"November 5, 1968
Dear Ma and Pa,

I'm in the hospital here in Viet Nam. I got hurt pretty bad and am in a body cast. They say that I'll be fine and will be sent back to the states in a few weeks. I think I'm going to a hospital in Texas.

How is the rest of the family? I really miss you all. Sure would like to taste some of Ma's corn bread. The food here is pretty bad since I get my meals in an IV bottle.

They said that I will be discharged when I get better so keep your eyes open for a job for me. I'm not sure what I'll be able to do though.

Well, that's about all for now. I'll write more when I can. Give a big hug to Ma.

All my love,
Johnny"

"There. They should have it in about a week."

"Thanks Sarge. Now for the hard one. I gotta have you write one to my wife."

"I didn't know you were married."

"Been married for almost six months now. We got married right before I left to come here. Ready?"

"Yup."

"Marta Davis, P.O. Box 923, Elk Garden, West Virginia. Are

ya ready?"

"Go ahead John."

"Dear Marta,

I got hurt pretty bad a while back and am in the hospital here in Viet Nam. They say that I'll be able to hold down a job, but some things will be a lot different. I don't want you to wait for me. I can't be the husband I was when I left and we'll never have a family. I want you to file for a divorce and start over again. Please don't look back. There's nothing here.
John"

As I finished the last sentence, I looked up and John had large tears rolling down his dark brown cheeks and into the plaster cast. Later he told me that during the surgery, they had removed most of his private parts. He felt that his marriage would wither and die anyway and it was best for them both to just end it now. This was a good man that had been dealt a bad hand and was playing it out the only way he knew.

A couple days later I awoke early one morning, still in the same hospital. I looked over to see if John was awake yet and he wasn't there. I asked the guy in the bed on the other side of me where he was and he said that John had died near midnight from an embolism. I didn't know what an embolism was, but he sure as hell was gone.

## Chapter: 2    I'm Leavin' on a Jet Plane

Time in that damned hospital seemed to creep by at an astonishingly slow rate. Each day contained a minimum of a hundred hours with each one lasting forever. The tiles on the ceiling each contained small holes. They ran in irregularly numbered lines horizontally and vertically. As close as I could figure, each one had 432 holes. There were 47 tiles going the long way and the short way was only 26. So with my extremely high degree of math knowledge, I came up with just over half a million holes. I counted them nearly five million times, and came up with the same number a couple times so I figured that I might just have figured it correctly.

When chow in an Army hospital is an event that you really look forward to, you just gotta know that something's wrong. I ate whatever they brought me, but usually waited until the guy next to me had tried it first. My momma didn't raise no fools. I figured if he tipped over right away, I might just want to eat that bogey bait I had hidden in my night stand instead.

My temperature refused to come down to normal and in

turn, the medical staff refused to consider letting me head back to the world. I think they were afraid I'd let loose some dreaded disease upon the population.

Letters from home were a rarity, but that was nothing new for me. It got to the point where mail call was about as welcome as last call at a bar. I had a wife in the states, but she had long since quit thinking of herself as being married. Not much of a loss, but just the same it was embarrassing to go home on leave and see the grins and hear some of the comments.

Letter writing continued for the troops that couldn't handle a pencil, but sometimes it got a bit difficult to handle. One day while on ward patrol, I found a gentleman that was a bit chewed up from an air crash. He was an Aussie and even in poor health, he had an amazing sense of humor. He was in a cast from the waist down and kept a raging fever going for several days. The outcome was touch and go and from one minute to the next, I just didn't know when he'd blink out. It broke one day early in the morning and his appetite returned. He kept the nurses running for quite a while just bringing him food. His name was Roger.

Roger as it turned out, was quite a cribbage player and on the rare occasion when his hands were devoid of food, we'd play cards. We only had one cribbage board in the ward so we'd have to wait until some other grunts gave it up. He kept the jokes going hour after hour.

One early morning I was awakened by a nurse wanting to

take my temperature. I was sweating heavily and had a hard time breathing. The stub of my leg was pounding hard and I knew that an infection was once again rearing its ugly head. The doctors came in to take a look at me and determined that I had gangrene. Another operation followed in just a couple hours.

The angels gathered around once more and one of them put the same Halloween mask on me. You had a good home but you left, you're right. Sound off, one two, sound off, three four, one two three, fo...

From the time that I left the ward until I awoke once again was only a couple hours. The remainder of the day was spent lounging around in my jammies, the blue and white variety that all the military patients wear. I would wake up just long enough to take a sip of water and then fall back asleep. I think the guy next to me ate my lunch and supper.

The next time I awoke, that same gorgeous nurse with the blue eyes was staring at me. She took the thermometer from my mouth and didn't say anything.

"I feel a little lighter on one side today." and I grinned at her.

"They took another section of your leg. And now for the good news. You still have your knee and that really is good news. The Doc said that you had a bad spot of infection in the stub and that's what kept your temperature from coming back down."

"Can I go home today?"

"You're a hard case Sergeant. Your temp has to stay normal

for a week and then we'll talk."

"Any idea where they'll send me?"

"Probably Illinois."

I had another IV stuck in my arm so that kept me from ward patrol for a whole week. Still my temperature wouldn't come back down to normal which meant that there was still something wrong. My appetite had gone down the tubes but I forced myself to eat some of each meal whether I liked it or not. Actually the only thing that kept me alive was the SOS, the only Army chow fit for human consumption, "shit on a shingle". I felt pretty safe eating the stuff and deep inside I knew that nobody ever dies with a load of that in his gut. Hail to the Army cooks.

The next week, I got rid of the needle and bag once more. That meant a resumption in the ward patrol. I was writing at least ten letters a day and the word was getting out. Each one had a little p.s. at the end which said that the letter was written by a grumpy old sarge. One day I got word that one of my customers wanted to see me, so after lunch I headed out to look him up.

"Here ya go Sarge. This is from my wife. She said to give you a big hug, but my reputation's at stake here ya know. You'll have to settle for a box of cookies and our thanks."

I opened the box and peeked inside. There was a bunch of popcorn for packing material and nearly a dozen furry green chocolate chip cookies. The humidity of that damned place would rot nearly anything. I thanked him and headed back with my package in my lap. I was amazed how nice these people were.

On coming back into my own ward, I was faced with about twenty guys that hadn't eaten anything homemade in a very long time. I didn't want anyone to know that they were rotten so I just pretended to keep them for myself. They sure gave me a lot of grief about that.

Blue Eyes was on the night shift so we sat around shooting the breeze for a while. Somewhere around midnight, she gave me the good news. The doctor had just signed my release to head back to the world. It was Illinois, just as we'd figured. First I'd go to the Philippines and then catch a C5A Medevac flight to the states. I was excited and a bit sad to leave my buddies, but more importantly leaving nurse Blue Eyes was really the pits. Hard to believe though since I didn't even know her first name. For weeks I had called her "Blue Eyes" and she called me "Sarge". It wasn't anything even close to being romance, but still, there was something there, something like being damned good friends.

"Ever been married?"

"Kinda." I said. "My wife isn't though."

"I think I might have heard this one before." she laughed.

I don't think she wanted to get into any kind of arrangement like that. Can't blame her either. She said that she'd been burned a while back when she found out that her roommate had a wife and a house full of kids. She pretty much quit looking at men.

"You been taking care of me for nearly two months now, and I still don't know your name."

She grinned and her face turned red.

"You gotta promise you won't tell a soul. OK?"

I nodded my head and she bent down to whisper in my ear. Her perfume damned near made me fall out of my chariot.

"Herman."

She straightened up and looked at me with a real serious look on her face. The laughter wanted to come out, but had me in a strangle hold around my throat. Then it came out, bursting forth with enough energy to awaken the entire ward.

I tried to quiet down, and when I looked at Blue Eyes, she wasn't even grinning. Damn. That's impossible. Nobody would ever name their girl Herman. Nobody.

Just then an alarm went off and she disappeared quickly into the adjoining ward, and out of my life. As I wheeled slowly back toward my ward, an old favorite song of mine was going through my head. "You must remember this. A kiss is still a kiss. A sigh is just a sigh. The fundamental things apply, as time goes by." The song, "As time goes by" ran through my head like a slow moving stream until I finally fell asleep.

The next morning I got my shaving kit and a few personal items thrown into a bag and was quite unceremoniously hauled outside into the South Viet Nam sunshine and a waiting army green ambulance. The heat and humidity were just as wonderful as the day I'd arrived here. The stretcher was hung on a rack with a few others and we proceeded to the airstrip near flight operations. There was a KC-135 tanker sitting there with ample room for a few broken down GI's. He had to make a trip to the Philippines, and that was right where I wanted to go. Anything that would get me closer to the states was alright by me. They loaded us on board and belted us down tightly for the trip. I got first class treatment and was able to see out a window.

After quite a while of just sitting, the engines came to life and the flying gas station started to move on the tarmac. As the aircraft turned toward the taxiway, I saw someone in white, standing by the doorway at base operations. I'd like to think that it was Blue Eyes.

The engines gave a great surge of power and the plane started down the runway, gathering speed as it went. Faster and faster and faster, and then the klaxon alarm went off. I looked out the window, a bit afraid of what I'd see. Rotation. The nose lifted and I know that if my arm had been just a wee bit longer, I could have picked off a palm branch. The alarm stopped and my heart gradually slowed down to a leisurely 180 beats per minute.

The lush green of Viet Nam was far prettier when watching it disappear out the rear view mirror. We turned left at the first stop light and went out over the water, gaining altitude. The ocean was blue green in the morning sun. All's right with the world. Damn you Viet Nam. Bye Herman. I'll miss you.

The trip there was pretty uneventful with all the GI's strapped into their stretchers. Once in a while an in-flight nurse would stop and see how we were. One was a guy from New York and he sure sounded a lot like Brooklyn. That is one accent that I've never forgotten.

He asked if I wanted to play a game of cribbage and even from a fully reclined position, I whupped him badly. He didn't seem to mind too much.

Landing in the Philippines was pretty uneventful. I must have been sleeping because the hard thud of the landing gear awakened me with a start. At first I couldn't think where I was. Then I remembered.

The wounded were unloaded into ambulances and transferred to the hospital grounds. I watched as the staff carried the stretchers, one by one inside the building. The guy right in front of me got a bad scare when one of the guys stumbled, nearly dropping him on the ground. It looked like those guys were just plain tired.

I was hungry enough to eat a horse. Air Force in-flight lunches consisted of a dried out sandwich and an apple. Those cooks were so damned creative. Now I wanted food, real food. By the time I got settled inside the new ward, it was almost 5:00 in the afternoon and that thin sliver of ham had worn off hours ago. The meal cart was rolled in and trays were passed around to each patient. Nothing for the four new guys though.

"What kind of shit is this?" I asked. "Get four meals in here and do it now. You hear me?"

The corpsman looked at me and just walked out of the ward. I gave him five minutes and then it started to sound a lot like

a string of mortars rounds going off in the ward. I grabbed
a coke bottle and threw it across the floor, breaking it on the
wall. Then I grabbed an empty IV bottle and threw that as well,
smashing it on the floor. That got some attention and a nurse
ran into the ward looking for the cause of all the noise.

"You got some hungry troops here, and if you don't have
chow in front of them in two minutes, I'm going to bust out
every window in this joint. You got that?"

The nurse turned and fled the scene, no doubt looking for
four trays of food. In a couple minutes, a doctor came into the
ward.

"Understand we got some hungry GI's here."

"You got it Doc and I'm about to start dismantling this
building. These men need to be fed and I mean right away."

"We're out of chow, but if you can wait for around 30
minutes, we ordered four T-Bone steak dinners from the
Officer's Club. I had to raid General Martin's private supply,
but I don't think he'll miss them. No charge of course."

He turned quickly and walked out of the ward. The other
guys were grinning from ear to ear. Steak! We hadn't seen a
real steak in one hell of a long time.

At the appointed time, the food showed up, covered tightly
to keep it hot. They handed us our trays and I opened mine to
find a huge steak smothered in onions and mushrooms. There
was another plate with mashed potatoes and gravy, and a small
bowl of peas. On the side there were two hard rolls and lots
of butter. Coffee and milk were added just to make the meal

complete. What a life! All I had to give for this fine meal was most of a leg.

We stayed there in that stinking ward for nearly a week. It must have been some kind of a staging area to get the wounded back to the states. It was extremely depressing and each day found new empty beds and full body bags. Some just couldn't last until breakfast and died during the night of their wounds. A steady stream of injured kept coming in. The hospital crew tried to stabilize them for shipment back home, but some just couldn't wait and went home early.

A really young looking GI named Tim took up residence in the bed next to mine. He was laying on his belly with a multitude of lines and hoses either going in or coming out of him. He slept a lot because of the big "M", the killer of all pain. They kept him so doped up that most of the time he didn't have any idea if he was on foot or horseback.

"Sarge?" he said softly. "I heard them call you Sarge." His eyes wandered around the room.

I rolled over and looked at him. His face looked so young to be here in this hole.

"Whatcha need soldier?"

His voice was so low that I had a hard time understanding what he was saying.

"I heard 'em say that you write letters."

"Ya. I do that sometimes. You need one written?"

"I got a girlfriend back home and I want to tell her I'm OK." he whispered.

"I think I can handle that. After supper alright with you?"

"Naw. We better do it now. After they change my dressing, I have a hard time talking for quite a while."

I got the pencil and paper out and wrote his words down as he whispered them to me. It was difficult to hear everything and sometimes he blinked out for a bit. We got the job done just as two doctors came in pushing a cart with a silver tray on top. They were there to change his dressing and it was a pretty tough job for all of us. I heard from a nurse what had happened to him. The back door had just dropped on their armored personnel carrier and a rocket propelled grenade round came in and hit him across the cheek of his ass. It split him open like a side of beef, but didn't explode. The doctors couldn't sew him back together yet because of infection, a normal problem for that filthy place. Twice a day they ripped off the gauze that stuck to his wound and put a fresh dressing on him. His screaming only stopped when his voice and strength gave out. There just had to be a better way to take care of him. When it was done, he couldn't even make a sound. Damned war!

The next few days were spent doing the job I had taken on for myself. Threatening to tear down the walls of this joint got me a little space and the chance to move around some. I went from ward to ward helping where I could and writing letters any time I was asked. On one occasion, a nurse handed me a note from the "A" Ward. It said that there was a gunnery sergeant there that wanted to see me. I mounted my chariot and wheeled down to see him.

He was in pretty tough shape and had a hard time speaking loud enough for me to hear.

"I need ya to write one for me Sarge."

"Sure. I got my stuff here with me. Who's it to?"

He started to give the address and I wrote down everything he said, listening closely so I wouldn't miss anything. The letter was to his parents in Wisconsin. He started by telling them that he was wounded and thanked them for all they had done for him. He sent his love to a whole bunch of people. Then he got some quieter and said that he didn't figure he'd make it home.

"Do you want me to write that in the letter?"

He nodded. Then he said that he wanted all his guns sent to his kids when they got old enough. I figured he must be married, but he never said anything about it. I looked up at him and he was sweating hard and his hands were shaking. He continued for another couple minutes.

"Guess that's about it Sarge." he said.

I told him that I'd mail the letter when I went by the mailbox in the ward. He managed a slight grin.

The next morning I woke up pretty early and decided to go and check on the gunnery sergeant. As I came into his ward, right away I saw that his bed contained a new occupant. The goddamned bed hadn't even cooled off and they had a new guy taking his place. Damned war!

Very early the next morning, a corpsman came around with the news that if we had normal temps, we'd be on the Medevac plane the next day, heading for the states. I was sick of this part of the world and the feeling was shared by everyone there.

The C5A Medevac plane was loaded with wounded stacked on stretchers everywhere. We all were pretty glad to be on the way home, but by the looks of the passengers, it was a sure thing that some wouldn't make it. The giant engines came to life and we rolled out onto the runway. Then the engines wound up hard and we left the jungles and war behind, heading for Elmendorf Air Force Base in Anchorage Alaska.

A few hours into the flight, they started to pass out the ever familiar in-flight lunches that the Air Force was so famous for. Some of the guys just handed them back and asked for a refund. It sure wasn't anything like the steaks we'd had earlier. After the big dinner, they turned down the cabin lights and some of us tried hard to get some sleep. Next to me, on the other side of the aisle, a GI was having a hard time breathing. Then he calmed down and went to sleep.

As we approached Anchorage for refueling, they turned up the cabin lights and checked everyone's safety belts. The young guy across from me had died and they just covered his face and continued on down the aisle checking the others. An event like this in any other time or place would bring a serious reaction from everyone, but on this day in the sky over Alaska, it didn't even get a second look. These were indeed hard times for us all.

The sound of the giant engines changed some and the plane banked slightly to the left giving me a good look at what was below us. We dropped slightly and leveled off for a time, the engines making a little less noise. I peeked again out the little window and we were getting closer to the runway. Outside of each window there was the spectacular view of mountains as far as I could see.

The landing gear touched the ground lightly and we rolled out almost to the end of the runway. I could see the waiting ground crew and then the door opened, letting in the first fresh air in a long time. The cold swept through the cabin, making everyone that was able, grab their blankets.

As they refueled the giant plane, a whole group of military wives came on board giving out cookies and coffee. Some had knitted small stocking caps to put over the ends of missing legs and arms. All of their efforts were sincerely appreciated, but the best part was to see their smiles. A friendly face is never forgotten.

While on the ground, they took the ones that hadn't made it and moved them into the cargo hold. I guess they didn't want to upset us. By the time we'd gotten this far, we'd seen worse than this, one hell of a lot worse.

The sight of the gigantic snow covered mountains made for a memorable flight. Using my more than fertile imagination, I could see Dall sheep, moose and caribou tramping through the fertile countryside, and all from 25,000 feet.

The flight on to Illinois was pretty uneventful. A little bumpy turbulence was about the only complaint and even an army chaplain couldn't have fixed that. The ones that were in bad shape had already died and the last of us were in good spirits as we came across the Canadian border and back into the states. A small cheer went up when the notice was given. For some of us, it had indeed been a long time. There were parents and kids to see and wives to be ravished. Funny how you can be away from your wife for so long and one roll in the hay makes it all forgotten. I wondered who had been taking my place, bless their sweet ass.

Illinois was clear and cold when we arrived and it seemed a bit strange to see the piles of snow on the runway. Jungle to snow banks in less than one day. I thought about Blue Eyes and wondered how she was and if she knew how to make a snowman. She'd probably never even seen snow.

They transferred us all to busses and then off to the Air Force hospital. The trip didn't take long, but it sure as hell was cold in there.

The wards were huge, but all the beds were a bit more private with curtains that you could pull around each bed. Not exactly home, but a definite improvement over Viet Nam. God what a variety of injuries there were in that place. When it comes to war, man's inhumanity to man knows no bounds. We are extremely creative in how we maim each other.

We had no more than gotten settled in the new beds than a nurse came around with our menus for the next day. The instructions were typed on the back of each one. "Circle what you want. If you want two, write a 2 beside it. If you want three, write a 3, etc. Just make sure you eat what you order." I looked over that menu and it was quite evident that the plane had taken a wrong turn somewhere. This was more like a fancy restaurant. You got whatever you wanted and more. I grabbed the pencil and started to circle stuff. I had seen some Army nurses, but this for damned sure wasn't an Army Hospital. The Army tries to kill you with their slop. Not these fly-boys. They eat pretty damned good. I was supposed to put the menu back on the evening meal tray when I was finished. I swallowed hard and started to draw circles. Coffee, milk, buttermilk, chocolate milk, toast(2), no tea, grits, oatmeal, eggs(3), bacon(4), sausage links(4) fried potatoes, french toast(2) syrup, salt, pepper, ketchup(3), sugar(4), butter(2) jelly(2). There, finished. Damn, I still had two more meals and an evening snack to go through. It was a tough job but somebody had to do it. I just kept drawing little circles on the paper.

The next morning the results of my overambitious nature became extremely evident. At 6:30 the big stainless steel cart was wheeled into the ward and each patient got the full order that they had made the day before. I sat up in bed and a good looking nurse sat a loaded tray on the table for me. She walked away and I figured that I had hit the mother lode for sure. There was more good food on this tray than I'd seen in the last two years. I took a stab at the sausage, but before I could get it into my mouth, the nurse had returned with the second load.

"Where should I put this one?" she asked.

I looked and it was nearly a duplicate load to the first one. I just pointed at the bed right next to me. She grinned and just stood there watching me.

"Think you can do it?"

"Not sure Ma'am." I said.

"Well, If you don't make it, at least you'll get a medal for trying."

She gave out a long laugh and went off to finish her appointed rounds. I ate slowly and almost polished off the whole thing, except that is, for the nice big apple. I never ordered no damned apple and dammit I wasn't going to eat it no matter what they said.

Lunch was served that day at 11:30. Supper was served at 5:15. Snacks were served at around 8:30. I never did that again.

## Chapter: 3    Maggie Marie Moore

The Viet Nam war had been pretty tough on Nurse Maggie.
When she arrived in country she was 25 years old and it took
quite a bit to rattle her. Nursing school had prepared her for
most things and her three year career in one of the toughest
parts of Los Angeles hardened her even more. Shootings, knife
attacks, rapes and accidents all came together to make her one
hell of a nurse.

A fading love affair with a young resident made her look
toward things like the Army or the Marines. She'd seen quite a
few ads on TV saying that they needed experienced nurses so
with a determination born of desperation she fled California for
a try at the Army and a new life. She was given the rank of first
lieutenant and a formal indoctrination into the "Army way" of
doing things.

Maggie grew up in the small village of Bear River,
Minnesota, a small town of around six hundred good people.
Graduation from high school was followed by another four
years of nursing school. By the time she finished that, she'd

seen enough of classrooms and crabby professors to last a lifetime. Methodist Hospital in L.A. handed her a contract as soon as she graduated. She was eager to get to work.

She was put on the perpetual night shift and that seemed to be the worst of all. The wounded came in by leaps and bounds. A full moon always brought out a fresh batch of suicide attempts. Drug overdoses and stabbings seemed to be her specialty. During her first week there, she was given two black eyes and a deep cut on her left forearm. It was a damned tough place.

During her first year at Methodist, she met a young intern that interested her. He found her to be extremely beautiful and she thought of him as the knight on the white charger. She eventually fell madly in love with him and that made two of them. He loved himself as much as Maggie and was extremely self centered. She gave him the option of taking a hike or just plain getting lost and since he had a hard time deciding, Maggie chose for him. She was a bit empty for a while, but just dove deeper into her job. Her devotion to duty got her many commendations.

Maggie was getting quite a reputation as being a loner. A daring young doc made a play for her and to his surprise, she accepted his invitation to dinner. It had been nearly two years since she had been on a date. After a dinner of steak and escargot they finished the evening dancing in a local night club. As the evening came to a close he drove her home and walked her to her apartment door. They awkwardly said thank you for the nice time and a small kiss that started innocently enough, blossomed, and grew into a night of gentle, urgent, very urgent lovemaking.

Even though she was determined not to let it happen, she became totally infatuated with this young man. In a months time, they were getting together as often as they could. Maggie was deeply in love, and her Romeo wanted nothing more or less than sex. Each time she broached the subject of a future, there was an audible closing of some unseen door.

"I see you're dating Jim Wilson." a nurse friend said one day.

"He's just wonderful and we really do get along well." said Maggie. "I just wish he didn't have to hold down two jobs. His student loans must be killing him."

"Maggie. There's something you just gotta know."

"Oh jeez. I hate this."

"Maggie, he's married and has one kid and his wife's pregnant. I just saw him the other day in the grocery store. I have a friend in personnel and she checked him out for me. He's married all right."

Maggie was shocked by this stunning revelation, too shocked to even cry.

"Thanks Mary."

Maggie hung her head as she walked along. It felt like she'd just lost her last friend. The sex they'd had felt an awful lot like real love, but that may have been in large part wishful thinking. Now she had some hard choices to make.

If she stayed on at Methodist, she'd be forced to see him. There was no way to isolate herself from him when they both worked in the same hospital. She had several weeks of vacation saved up and walked into personnel trying to claim three weeks for herself and right away. It must have been just the perfect time to put in for time off, because she was given her vacation and it started right then and there. She thanked her lucky stars that she didn't have to chance seeing "him" before she left. That "him" just might have gotten his head knocked off.

As she walked back into her apartment, the phone was ringing and then the answering machine picked it up.

"Maggie. Tell me what's wrong. You don't return my phone calls and now I heard that you're on vacation. Call me at the hospital."

She thought for a moment whether she should call him at his home and wreck his marriage or maybe just forget the whole thing and go on. She chose the latter and never looked back.

Bear River, Minnesota didn't have any direct air connections or even a grass airstrip, so when she got to Duluth, she rented a car and drove the last hundred miles of the trip stopping into a small store to buy some groceries for her folks. She always felt better if she brought something.

As the trip continued, she started to think of what she could do with the rest of her life. Romance was wonderful, but the thoughts of marriage and children just weren't in her big picture right now. She pulled into the yard and saw several cars there and a few parked out on the street. She walked into the house and looked around for her Mom and Dad. Just then her Dad walked into the kitchen and saw her. He broke into tears and went to Maggie to give her a hug.

"Maggie. Mom just died a couple hours ago. She must have had a stroke while she was sleeping. I tried to call you, but all I got was your answering machine."

Tears filled her eyes and she held onto her Dad for all she was worth. It felt like she was in deep water and going down for the third time. Maggie and her Mom had been very close. She cried hard for several minutes and her Dad just held her softly. In the living room was her brother and his family with several cousins and neighbors. Everyone really loved her Mom and it showed.

Her Dad was a retired lawyer and a pretty self sufficient man and she knew he could take care of himself. It would be hard, but at the age of 60, he could do most things for himself.

The funeral brought out nearly the whole town and when it was over they went back to the church for a small meal and conversation. A couple friends cornered her and asked what she had been doing. She told about her job in Los Angeles and that seemed to be enough for them. No questions about her lovers and many many romances.

The following Monday, she drove into Grand Lake and stopped to see the Army recruiter. He promised her just about everything but breakfast in bed each Saturday. The pay would be quite a bit less, but at that point in her life, money was the least of her worries. The next day she brought in all of her credentials and diplomas and the recruiter had already gotten the OK to accept her. Not being one to waste time, she agreed to start her hitch in 30 days. That gave her time to go back and clear out her apartment. She also had to give notice at the hospital. She figured that about a three hour notice would be sufficient. She called in and gave them the news. To her surprise, the administrator was extremely supportive and said that he'd help in any way he was asked. That took a load off her shoulders. He even thanked her for her years of helping the hospital grow and prosper.

After a hurried trip to L.A. to clean out the apartment, she decided to rent a car and drive back to Minnesota. She stopped in at the travel agency and with their help, mapped out a course that lead her through Las Vegas for a little gambling, Yellowstone Park, and then Mount Rushmore. She had never seen these parts of the country and was enthralled by their beauty. Each night she found herself in a different motel and eating in a different restaurant. In Cody Wyoming, she ran into a couple girls about her age. They were sitting in the pool area of a local motel drinking Margueritas so Maggie just went up and introduced herself. They were driving to Wisconsin and seemed to be very friendly.

After two drinks, Maggie and the others started to talk about picking up some men. She wasn't sure this was such a good idea, but said that she'd go along and watch. With that, they left for a local bar. There was a country band playing and line dancing was the order of the day. She'd never even seen that before and learned as she went along. She was having a good time and looked up just in time to see her two new friends leave with a couple cowboys in tow. It sure didn't take them long. Well, that left her alone against the whole rest of the world's man population. A couple guys asked her to dance and it started to get a bit too intense for her. She excused herself to go to the ladies room and slipped out the door. There was a taxi there so she just jumped in and went back to her motel. That was about all the fun she could handle for one night. By 11:00 she was back in her room, sound asleep.

Around noon the next day, she was headed back toward Minnesota, feeling a bit worse for wear. She'd had a good time and found out that she liked line dancing.

When she got back home, she found a spot to store most of her belongings. Her Dad was sorry to see her leave and cooked a big dinner for her on the last night home. All he could give for advice was to be careful. He never bothered to tell her what she should be careful of, but she figured it was intended to make her careful in all situations. Inside she appreciated how her Dad still tried to protect her.

Maggie was supposed to be at the Federal Building in Minneapolis the next day at 5:30 a.m. for her formal introduction to the Army. There was a long line of guys there being inducted and they were being treated like shit, especially after they took their oath of service. Then they belonged to Uncle Sam and he could kill and eat them if he wanted to.

Maggie on the other hand was treated in a more professional manner and introduced to a couple medical officers. They told her about what she needed to do for the next few weeks and what it would be like. She had to learn customs and courtesy and especially how to march. She had to learn weapons and that bothered her some, but her Dad had taken her hunting since she was seven years old, and guns were nothing new to her. Here she was, a trained nurse and they were going to teach her how to kill people. How ironic!

The whole Army experience was looked upon as being just another thing to be enjoyed. She had no idea that she could run five miles. In the six weeks she was in training, she started to love the whole thing. Three meals a day and all the good looking men she could handle. Could it get any better than this?

At the time of her graduation, the Viet Nam war was going strong. Her intentions when she joined the Army were to help in the war and she wasn't going to be disappointed. As she and a couple friends opened their orders, it seemed that they were all headed in the same direction. Southeast Asia would have a brand new team of nurses to care for the wounded.

Maggie was given the opportunity to go home on leave for a couple weeks, but wanted to get on with her new career. She was given her plane tickets to San Francisco and would catch an Air Force plane to Hickam Air Force Base in Hawaii and then straight to Taiwan. From there she'd have to wing it on her own and just catch the first plane to her new base. Taiwan was a filthy place and it stunk like somebody had forgotten to flush.

It was snowing hard when she got there, but it was melting as fast as it hit.

She saw a group of people hauling dirt in baskets, like they'd done for so many centuries, balanced on their heads. It seemed so strange to be surrounded by all of the tools of the twentieth century and just outside it was still 300 A.D. She spent just one night there and then she got a hop into Viet Nam.

A C-47 with a new facelift carried her the rest of the way to Viet Nam. It was the new one called "Puff" as in Puff the magic dragon. When this bad boy spoke, things either broke or burned. It seemed to have guns everywhere. The flight crew all wanted her address and phone number and she felt flattered.

As she got some closer to her base, they gave her a tour of the place. The plane came down low to the jungle canopy and with engines revving in high gear, gave her a good look at the countryside. Even from there she could tell it was hot and steamy.

First stop near noon was supply to pick up her blankets and sheets. The temp was almost a hundred and so was the humidity. She was sweating profusely and some guy was handing her army green woolen blankets. She silently wondered what the hell she would need them for but in a few days she was covering up like everyone else.

Rain and mud seemed to be the order of the day, every day. She was housed in a 20 bed hootch along with a bunch of other nurses. She arranged for a house-girl and got settled in. The hootch was nothing more than a building frame with screen walls. The corrugated steel roof made a hell of a racket each time it rained. Mosquitoes were a constant problem until she got a net to put over her bed. One night as she was trying to fall asleep, she caught a movement out of the corner of her eye. A small lizard was scrambling around eating any kind of bug it could catch. He was light green and actually quite pretty.

Her duty station was surgery and triage, just the sort of thing she had hoped for. Her previous training had prepared her for the rapid pace of this war. She would go back to her hootch each evening not knowing when she would be called in again. She was on duty 24 hours a day.

The Army mess hall was nearly half a mile away and she had to walk over a small creek to get to it. The rotting vegetation from the water nearly made her loose her lunch a couple times. It took quite a while just to get used to the smells. Army chow wasn't fit for human consumption so she ate most of her meals out of a can. There was Vienna sausages, tuna, hot dogs cooked over an alcohol lamp; she became quite creative and kept away from the chow hall as much as possible.

One afternoon she and a couple others were sitting around talking and she saw a gal at the other end of the hootch take a glass of water and pour some scotch into it. It wasn't much, but she drank it right down.

"Julia!" someone yelled. "Isn't it a bit early for scotch?"

"It's the only way you can drink the water." she said. "Try it."

Maggie went over and helped herself. The water was

usually pretty gross and she drank Pepsi and 7 Up instead. She poured a glass of water and then added a bit of Julie's scotch. She tasted it and found that it was actually pretty good. All the rest joined in and pretty soon a couple went back for seconds. Within an hour the hootch was transformed into a giggling mass of nurses, all in love with scotch whiskey. There was absolutely nothing that wasn't funny. Julia had turned a rainy humid afternoon into party time. The music was turned up loud and the party continued for hours.

Around 10 p.m. the duty phone rang and they needed five nurses in surgery right away. They had several wounded coming in by chopper in a half hour, just enough time to shower and dress. That sobering thought ended the party, but they all had fun while it lasted.

After Maggie had been in country a few months, she started to get out once in a while and do some shopping. She found restaurants that served seafood and things she'd never even heard of. She loved stir fried vegetables with fish sauce and fried rice with pork. Her and a friend had finished their dinner one afternoon and decided to walk back to their hootch a couple miles away.

As they walked along, they were greeted by many people all trying to sell something.

"What is that terrible smell?" asked Maggie.

"Beats me." said her friend. "The whole place stinks as far as I'm concerned."

"No. This is different."

Her friend started laughing. Right next to the road was a barrel sitting on a stand. A man was climbing a short ladder to reach the top and then lifted the lid. He poured in a bucket of small fish and then came back down.

Her friend just kept laughing.

"Remember that fish sauce you like? Go over there and open that valve and you can have all you like. All that fish is rotting in the sunshine and what comes out of the bottom is the stuff you like so much."

She changed her mind about the fish sauce.

One afternoon she and her pal Mary went to the town on a shopping trip and had just finished their lunch. Monks were sometimes hired to come and bless a certain business and they would sit outside in a row, praying. Just as they went past, they heard the sound of people talking loudly and turned back to see a Monk pouring something over his head. He walked to the middle of the street and snapped open his Zippo. One small spark was all it took and he was on fire burning brightly, writhing on the ground and not making a sound. Nobody moved to help him and just let him burn until he was dead. There wasn't anything that they could do to help so they moved quickly out of the area and headed back to base. Life was so damned cheap here.

Maggie started to hear the word "Tet" once in a while and within a few weeks she knew what it meant. She didn't need an alarm clock to awaken her each morning. Usually a short rocket attack did the trick. It was only a few rounds but enough to keep everyone on edge for hours. The "Tet" offensive had begun and the wounded were coming in by the dozens. Her skills as a nurse were put to the test each day but the sheer volume of wounded was overwhelming.

One afternoon as the dust was starting to settle, she stood in a corner looking around to see what needed to be done next. Who needed care most? Who needed pain killers? Who needed their IV bag changed? Then she started to cry. The whole thing just came on her like a flood. She was totally overwhelmed, and the tears flowed like a river. She sat down in a private corner and just let it come out. A surgeon friend saw her and came in to offer support.

The next morning she was moved to the wards. No nurse can stand to see the carnage she had and do it day after day. If she was to remain in nursing, she'd have to move around some to take the pressure off.

After a short while she got to really like nursing in the wards. It challenged her skills both as a nurse and as a human. There seemed to be so darned many young men that would never be the same again. Their transition back to civilian life would be hard. Some had lost limbs. Some were blind.

The months came and went. She found her nursing skills growing and she was developing into the person she would be for the rest of her life. She now had a new tool at her disposal and it's name was "compassion". She was able now to help the patients on nearly any level they needed. Her twelve month assignment in Viet Nam was nearing an end.

## To Waltz With A White Horse

She'd been taking care of a sergeant and he'd started calling her blue eyes. She was starting to have feelings for him and kept him at a distance. One evening as most of the patients were sleeping he rolled up to the nursing station in his wheelchair. They talked for a long time and he had asked her name.

## Chapter: 4   Illinois

Life in the hospital was starting to get to me. After several weeks there, my fevers came and went with still no idea of what was causing them. The end of my stump always looked red and sore. I had another memento of Viet Nam and that was a small shrapnel wound on my left arm. In my first surgery, they removed a small piece of metal and gave me a stitch or two and that was the end of it. Now the arm was always in pain and I found it difficult to get it in a comfortable position. Too much time to think had me worrying about losing the arm. It was one thing to lose the foot, but a far different problem to lose another limb. Each time the Doc came in to check me, he looked with suspicion at my temperature chart. He figured there was another operation in the offing.

One Sunday evening I was talking to another GI about the war and he said that it didn't bother him in the least.

"I take as much of this place as I can and then I take some shit to get me through 'til the next day." he said.

"How do you get it here in the ward?" I asked him.

"I got a friend that brings it to me. I give him a ten spot and he takes care of me."

"I been having a lot of pain and if I ask for more meds, they'll chop more of my leg off. Can ya get me some?"

"Sure. Got the money?"

I reached in my pajama pocket and pulled out a $10.00 bill.

"When can you get it?"

"I'll have it here tomorrow morning."

I was pretty worried about getting caught, but the alternative was pretty bad too. Six of one, half a dozen of another. A pill or two to take the edge off wasn't so terrible.

The next day the stuff was there as advertised. He handed me a small package and I tucked it in my pj's. Later I went to the latrine and sat down in a stall to examine my purchase. It was white powder and I wasn't sure what to do with it. I wrapped it up and went back to the ward. I found my supplier and in private questioned him.

"Now, what the hell do I do with this stuff?"

"You put it in a spoon with some water and cook it. Then you inject it into a vein." he laughed. "You sure are green for a sergeant."

"I never messed with this stuff before and don't give me your crap. Hear me?"

"I'll give you a hand with the first load, but don't ask me to do it again."

After chow that night, we agreed to meet in the latrine at the end of the hall. We went into a wheelchair stall and my new friend introduced me to the wonderful world of the horse. He had a candle stub, a spoon, and a brand new syringe. They were quite easy to come by here. He had done this a million times and in short order, the horse was ready to ride. He wrapped a piece of rubber around my upper arm and then told me to make a fist. A good vein popped up and he moved the needle into position.

"Sure ya wanna do this?" he asked.

"It's either this or the operating room."

Very slowly the needle entered my body, then he pushed the plunger. The heroin was in and now all that was left was to remove the rubber band from my arm. It went from my arm to my heart and then into my brain and I could feel it start. It was making me a little dizzy at first and then a feeling of "I just don't give a shit" came over me. My new friend was putting his tools away and then he left me sitting there in the stall, all alone, staring at the wall. Pain? What pain! At that moment in time, they could have cut an arm off without any anesthesia and I'd have thrown in a leg steak just for kicks.

After a couple hours of just sitting there, I decided to head back to the ward. I wheeled toward my bed, but I got lost. I left it right there. Now where the hell is my bed? Now how the hell does a guy lose a bed? I laughed a little and a nurse looked at me.

"Ya lost Sarge?"

"I guess I must have taken a wrong turn. Where's my ward?"

She pointed down the hall the other direction and that was

enough to get me home for the night. I lay there in bed for quite a while thinking. This was the best I'd felt in one hell of a long time. This horse and I were going to be best buddies.

The next morning I awoke about two hours after breakfast. My tray was sitting on the table and it looked pretty gross. Cold oatmeal has little appeal to anyone. I was having some trouble focusing my eyes, but I figured it was from the shit I had done. I just wasn't a bit sure what the side effects were for that stuff. My arm was throbbing some and my leg still ached like a toothache.

I wheeled over to the nurses station and asked if there was any coffee around. A little dark haired nurse showed me the way to the nurses lounge. There was a two year supply there even though it was several hours old. Too bad you can't take coffee injections. It'd save a lot of dirty dishes.

Wednesdays were the day of the week when the new group of wounded would come in and I wanted to see if there were any from my old company. None this time, but I did see a guy that I knew from Nam. His name was Phil something or other and he was grunt like me. We talked for a while and then they came and got him, to show him his new ward. He was on the fifth floor, right below me. We agreed to meet later when I made my rounds.

My letter writing had taken on the looks of being a full time job and that was OK with me. Today it was the 3rd floor. I took the elevator and rode down with one of the Docs. He was a pretty nice guy and asked how I was doing.

"OK sir but I sure would like to go home some day."

"Well, as soon as they see that you're stabilized, they'll give you at least 30 days of convalescent leave."

"That would be great." I said.

The door opened and I wheeled down the hall just a few feet and right into a young GI sitting in the hallway crying. He was sobbing hard and I asked him what the problem was. He jumped up and ran away down the hall. Then when he came to the end of the hall, he turned around and came right back in front of me. He just continued to run and then he fell down and sobbed some more. A nurse came up to him and he took off again.

"What the hell's wrong with him?" I asked her.

"His urinary tract is shut down and he can't urinate. He needs a catheter and won't let anyone put one in. His bladder is about to bust and he's in a lot of pain." she said.

"Let me have a try."

I went to where he was laying on his bed and grabbed his hand. He tried to pull away, but I had a good grip on him.

"What's your name?"

I looked him directly in his blue eyes. He couldn't have been much more than eighteen.

He looked back at me and said, "Jerry sir.".

"Jerry, ya need to get this taken care of and I'm gonna go in with you."

I still had a good grip on him and he tried hard to get away. I pushed him back on the bed and told him not to move.

"You stay right here, and that's an order."

He looked at me for a moment like he was going to take off again, but then a look of resignation crossed his face. It was time to face the inevitable.

I turned and wheeled back to the nurses station.

"Nurse. I'm gonna bring him in to get that catheter. I want a Doctor to do it and I'll be here in exactly three minutes. You be ready. Got it?"

I turned and wheeled back to get Jerry. I grabbed his hand again and told him that we were going to do this together. He looked like he was about to panic and then he just relaxed.

"Push me back down to the nurses station. I'm pretty tired." I said.

He got behind me and away we went. By the time I got there, a Doc was waiting and motioned for us to follow him. We went into the operating room and Jerry moved slowly up onto the table, agony written all over his young face. His pain was almost more than he could bear. The Doc opened the catheter kit and hooked it to a bag. Then he quickly inserted the catheter before Jerry could even think about it. The urine flowed into the bag like a river and Jerry's pain went away almost as fast. Within fifteen minutes, he was sitting in a wheel chair next to me in the hallway. We talked for quite a while and I found out that he was from Minnesota too. Small world I thought. These hospitals can be pretty scary places. In that short time of anger, fear and confusion, the young GI made another friend, a one legged grunt.

My duties for the day had long since been forgotten, and the pain in my arm and leg seemed to be getting worse all the time. I looked up my supplier and bought a hundred bucks worth. That should last me for as long as I was gonna be there. I just had to get better and go home for a while. This time I didn't have to wait for my shit. He had it in his pocket. I had gotten the needed equipment and went to a remote area to find some privacy. I cooked up a load and sucked it into a syringe. Then just as I had seen, I wrapped the band around my arm and found a vein. Sticking the needle in was a different story. It seemed that I had to work up the courage to do it. I sat for a while thinking and then just decided to do it. I stuck it in and ever so slowly pushed the plunger. The horse came alive and I could feel all of my cares and problems just walk away from me.

Again I sat for quite a while, feeling the effects of the heroin. It was kinda good and kinda scary at the same time. I didn't take too much because of the nurses watching me.

The next afternoon I cooked up another batch and it got a lot easier. This time I thought I'd use a little more than before.

"Have you seen Sarge?" a nurse asked the Doctor.

"I spose he's around somewhere writing letters."

"He didn't eat his lunch and now it's supper time."

"I wouldn't worry too much about him. He's pretty darned reliable."

Around midnight the whole hospital was looking for me. I was sitting in the morgue looking at a corpse hanging by a hook in the back of his head. They said that I was crying, but I don't remember that.

The Doc came in around six the next morning and shook me. He pulled up my left sleeve and looked at the injection marks.

"Where'd you get the dope?" and he sure as hell wasn't grinning.

I told him that I didn't know what he was talking about, but he was persistent. He told me about getting hooked on the stuff and then just left me to think about it for a while. If I quit taking the stuff, I'd never get home. I'd just have to be more careful.

The nurse said that my temperature had been steadily climbing and it was time to find out what was causing the problem. I was scheduled for surgery the next morning at 9:00. They were going to open up my stump again and irrigate it. I was pretty concerned that they might remove the knee. Without that, I'd be in shit shape in a hurry.

At 8:30 they came and got me with a gurney. I wasn't too sure I'd like this, but my friend Jerry was there for moral support. I had to put on a good face for him. He figured that he owed me one.

The angels gathered once more and put the Halloween mask on me. Ninety-nine, Ninety- eight, ninety-sev. The surgery lasted for a little more than an hour and I was back in the recovery room. I opened my eyes and figured that I'd made the trip again. I'd recover in a few days and be back to my abnormal self. I wouldn't need the dope any more. I fell asleep once again.

When I awoke back in my bed, I needed to know what they had found. My knee had disappeared and now it was tough times for the Sarge. Damned war. How the hell was I going to get along without a knee. Depression set in and became my ever constant companion. I was having a hard time and didn't quite know which way to turn. The only friend I could talk to was "The Horse".

One afternoon I cooked up a batch and it seemed to help quite a bit. That started me on extremely regular trips to the latrine to shoot up.

One afternoon as I lay in bed sleeping, I felt someone touch my arm and I instinctively pulled away. The small wound in my arm was leaking through the cloth and she had seen it. That started a round of inquiries on what had happened and then another trip to the operating room. I was getting to be a regular in there.

They opened it up and found a small piece of shrapnel they'd missed in Nam. The whole area was infected and they cut away quite a bit of my arm. When I woke up, there was a small drain tube coming from the incision. This whole thing was getting to be a lot like a bad dream. I just had to go home for a while.

I thought about home for a long time that day. In reality, there wasn't anything there for me. I hadn't heard from the little lady for nearly half a year.

# To Waltz With A White Horse

The drain tube and the IV bottle kept me from going into the latrine for a whole week. The cravings I had for heroin started to ease some by the fifth day. They took all the tubes out and that left me free to wander the wards again. Depression was once again rearing its ugly head, but this time I fought it off. No more damned drugs for me.

Another week went by with no word on when I was going home. When I talked to the Doc, he said that I wasn't ready. That set me off once more. That evening I headed to the latrine and loaded up again. It had been over a week and I needed it bad. This time it had little effect on me other than to make me feel better and that was bad. I started to ride the horse twice a day and the result was spending a ton of money on heroin. How could I go from a non-user to an addict so quickly? It happens all the time. My hundred bucks worth had disappeared a long time ago.

My supplier got sent home on convalescent leave and with him went the only supply of drugs I knew. After a couple days of abstinence, I was getting desperate. One night around 2 a.m. I wheeled down to the nurses station and broke into the drug cabinet. As I was going back toward my ward, a nurse caught up with me.

"What are you going to do with that stuff?"

"What stuff?"

"You know damned well what stuff. Do I have to call security to have you searched?"

She had the look of one of those old drill sergeants I had run into in the past.

"No."

"You get help or I turn you in. Got it? Now give me back the drugs."

I dug into my pockets and pulled out a hundred loose Percodan tablets. It seemed kind of strange. Just a couple months ago I didn't even know what drugs were.

Through the course of the next several weeks I struggled hard to overcome the painful urges to take drugs but once in a while I'd go to the latrine and shoot up. It seemed that there was always someone to sell me what I wanted. I tried hard to use as little as possible. It seemed that if I waited too long though, it took more to get the same high. I used up most of the money I had each month on drugs, but no matter how strung out I got, I never stole from the hospital again. That was as close as I'd ever been to trouble in my entire career.

One afternoon as I made my rounds, I came to a new guy that had the shakes pretty bad. I looked at him and recognized him as being one of the guys from my old platoon. He was Barry Jenkins and we'd been in some serious drinking tournaments in Nam. If I remembered right, I had won.

Barry was shaking like a dog shitting razor blades and when I touched his hand, he pulled back like he'd been burned.

"Barry. It's me Barry."

"Sarge?"

"Ya. What the hell's wrong?"

"I'm kinda strung out Sarge. I been doing a lot of heroin and now I'm out of money."

He had the look of a cornered animal.

"Damn. The monkey is on my back too, but I shot up a while ago and I'm OK for now."

"Can ya lend me some?" he asked with a pleading sound in his normally gruff voice.

"I don't know Barry. Look, I'll make you a deal. I'll go cold turkey with ya. We'll crash and burn together. I got about $50.00 worth of it and I'll flush it right here in front of ya."

"That might make you feel better, but it's not going to help me much. I need a fix now dammit." said Barry.

"They got a treatment center right here and we can do it together."

"I don't know about that Sarge."

"Listen. We both know that we gotta stop this bullshit, so you help me and I'll help you. If I remember right, you have a gorgeous wife and a couple kids. The last thing they want to see walk through the door is a worthless, piece of shit junkie."

I looked at him closely and tears came cascading from his eyes. He never made a sound, but just the same, he was at that moment, a broken man.

"What do ya think Barry?"

"Lock n load Sarge."

"I'll call the rehab center and they'll send somebody up here to talk to us."

The rest of the day went by pretty fast. We had a lot of papers to sign and schedules to write up. This clinic was pretty damned experienced since most of the patients came from a 12 month tour of Viet Nam. Damned War!

The next morning we had breakfast with the other junkies and I was damned surprised at how many of us there were. A lot of them only had wounds in the brain, but there were some Purple Hearts there too. We both found a bit of comfort knowing that there were so many others, just in this one hospital, that had problems. We had speeches to listen to and Methadone to take at regular intervals. That stuff was nearly as good as heroin. After a couple weeks, I found myself in a small room with some other losers, making purses out of leather. Some guys were painting and some of them were reading. We all had one thing in common though, we were all junkies.

My wounds were healing pretty well and there was still the thoughts in my mind of going home. My old man was still alive somewhere in Northern Minnesota and the last I heard, he was living up on the Bigfork River in a little cabin. Sure would be nice to see him, if I could catch him sober some time.

One morning the Doc came in and asked if I was ready to grow a new leg yet. The tenderness had eased some and I thought it might just work. I was fitted for a leg with a joint that moved. It would take some time to get used to it, but eventually, I knew I could do it.

Drug rehab classes were starting to have the desired effect and I was down to just a small amount of Methadone each day. Barry wasn't doing quite as well and still needed large doses of the stuff. They taught us that once you were a user, you were

always right on the edge of a relapse and that was a damned
scary thought. In my heart though, I knew they were right.

# Chapter: 5    Duty Site: CONUS

Maggie was coming to the end of her tour of duty and looked for her orders to come in every day. They could have sent her to almost anywhere in the continental United States. She walked to the mail room one afternoon and the large envelope she had waited for was there. She started to open it, but decided to take it back to the hootch. As she walked along, she had thoughts of going to some tropical place or maybe the frozen north of Alaska. Her talents could be used nearly anywhere there were troops. She sat on her bunk and tore the end open.

"On March 17, 1969, you will proceed to Chanute AFB, Illinois, being assigned to the 1423rd Medical Wing. Thirty days of annual leave granted. Report for duty April 27, 1969 at 0700 hrs." etc. This was where they sent Sarge. She started to smile. It sure would be good to see this old grunt again. He was the only man that had caught her attention in quite a while.

Her last two weeks in Viet Nam went by in a hurry. She had shopping to do, sending gifts to all of her family. She had to arrange for housing in Illinois at the Bachelors Officer Quarters. From there she would find an apartment and a car.

The last week of duty she didn't need to report in each morning. She had things to take care of. She was definitely a short-timer. Not even enough time for a whole cigarette. A friend handed her a pack of Pall Malls that had been cut in half and the pack put back together. Short timers smokes. She didn't smoke, but kept the gift.

Her Commanding Officer left her a note to report to the Officers Club on Saturday evening at 7:00. This was the big party she didn't want to have, lots of tears and long good-bye's. She walked in at a couple minutes before the appointed time and was greeted by a hundred or more friends and patients. They all cheered loudly as she walked in. Somewhere during the evening, the commander handed her the new double silver bars that meant she was now a Captain.

Maggie had to catch her plane at 1100 hours the next day and it was still up in the air at 0600 whether or not she'd be able to walk that far. She'd had a couple too many drinks and was poured into her hootch at midnight. She figured that she might have had a good time, but she wasn't sure.

She arrived at Base Ops an hour before her flight and sat in a dark corner trying to hide from the sunshine. Her head pounded loudly with each step she took. Good thing that she'd found a few barf bags to take with her. She'd probably need them. She took a motion sickness pill and a couple APC's in hopes that she'd make it back to the world alive.

As she sat there waiting, she thought of the old Sarge and wondered inside what he'd been up to. She also wondered if he'd remember her.

The loudspeaker called out "Captain Maggie Moore report to the front desk."

She struggled to her feet and walked up to see what was going on.

"You can board that KC-135 tanker over there. They'll be leaving in about a half hour."

She thanked him and went to get her carry-on bag. This was it, the end of stinking Viet Nam. Damned sure won't miss this place she thought.

She found a seat and settled in for the flight. Soon the engines revved up and they started to roll out onto the runway. She peeked out the window wondering if anyone had come to wave goodbye like she'd done for Sarge. She saw only the ground crew.

In just a few minutes, she was out over the ocean, heading for home. It sure would be nice to see her Dad again. It had been over a year but it seemed like a lot longer. Bear River, Minnesota seemed so darned far away. In reality it was a mere 13,000 miles, give or take a few, half way around the world. The plane kept gaining altitude for a long time and then leveled off. They were indeed on their way home, just a few more days.

Maggie arrived in Bear River, Minnesota four days after leaving Viet Nam. Her Dad was pretty glad to see her and invited all the relations to a big dinner. There were so many people that there was hardly room to sit. Dad had invited his new girlfriend and it felt terrible to think that he had already replaced Mom. She was a year older than her Dad and they seemed to do a lot of laughing and smiling. He looked way too darned happy. She was determined that she wasn't going to like that woman, but as the evening wore down to the final few people, she came over and sat by Maggie..

"It sure is nice to meet you Maggie." she said.

"You too Molly. It's good to see Dad so happy."

"He went through some really hard days after your Mom passed away. He felt so very lost. I lost my husband a short time before your Mom died and I knew what he was going through."

"I'm really sorry to hear that."

"Thanks Maggie. But there is something that you have to know. I'm not trying to replace your Mom. It could never be done. Your Dad and I are nothing more than friends and I'm pretty sure that's all that it will ever be."

That took a load off Maggie's mind. She was still a bit suspicious, but she was a little more at ease now. Molly really was a nice person.

On her second night home, her Dad came in and watched TV with her for a time. It seemed that he almost had to duck when he went through a doorway. He was way over 6 ½ feet tall and looked like a football player. His hair was nearly gone, but somehow, he still looked young.

"You feel like paddling a canoe tomorrow?" He was grinning from ear to ear.

"Sure!"

"I was thinking that maybe we could paddle around Deer Lake. That will take most of the day. You think you're up to it?" he asked.

"I can still run five miles without stopping. I hope you can keep up." she grinned.

The next morning after breakfast, they loaded the canoe and headed off to Deer Lake. The temperature was a balmy 60 degrees and the sky a bright burning blue. When they got to the lake the whole place was beautiful and extravagantly decorated with flowers and brightly colored birds. The water was calm and you could see way down to the bottom where the really big fish lived. They paddled slowly, not wanting to make any waves. Maggie sure had missed Minnesota.

"Look over there." said her Dad, excitement written in each word..

Maggie looked to where he was pointing and saw a huge fish sitting very still in the weeds. He was waiting for his breakfast to be served to him.

"Are you and Molly thinking of getting married?"

"Well, we talk of it once in a while. We're both pretty lonely. That house seems so darned big sometimes. If you sit real still you can hear a mouse fart from all the way across the room."

"You must have good ears." she laughed. "Or really big mice."

"She invites me over for dinner about five days a week and the other two, I ask her to dinner. I guess we do spend a lot of time together."

"Sounds serious."

"I think it could be, but it just doesn't seem right when your Mom died such a short time ago."

"Life is short Dad. If it feels right, it just might be the right thing to do."

"When you live in such a small town, you have to think of what the neighbors would say too. We don't want to upset the old village gossips you know."

Around noon, they paddled over to an island with a sandy beach. They had brought sandwiches and coffee and that was lunch. They sat watching the world go by and it seemed so much like when she was a kid. Her Dad always took her along on anything he did outdoors. She was his constant companion.

"Ready to paddle some more Maggie?"

"Sure am."

They continued paddling down the lake and a light breeze came up out of the west. Then in just a few minutes they heard thunder and that meant an approaching storm.

"We better head for the car Maggie. Let's see how tough you are."

With that, they headed back to the landing, paddling hard. It was only a couple blocks away, but before they got there, the rain had started, soaking them thoroughly. They got the canoe tied on and headed back home.

"Thanks Maggie. That's the most fun I've had in years."

"Me too Dad. I have often wondered how many miles you and I have paddled together." and she grinned.

Her leave went by at an astonishing rate and before she knew it, it was time to make plane reservations. She felt that her Dad now had a fighting chance with so many good friends. The last evening home, they went out to dinner together and her Dad was as cheerful as ever.

The next day she was on a plane heading southward to Illinois. She landed in Chicago and took a bus the rest of the way to Champagne - Urbana Illinois. She called the Motor Pool for a bus into the base. She got off at the B.O.Q. and registered. The building was barren of any decorations and not the kind of place she'd want to live in for long. After she settled in, she called her orderly room to say she had arrived. She had brought her uniforms with her and was ready for duty the next day, all she had to do was iron them.

The next morning she reported to the Commander as ordered. He welcomed her and personally gave her a tour of the hospital. It was 12 floors high and nearly full of wounded. The Commander asked her what she would like to do since she was now a Captain. This gave her a little freedom as to what kind of duty she would be doing. She decided that she'd like to be back on the wards, like she'd done in Viet Nam. The Commander did the necessary paper work and she started at 0700 the next morning.

Life on the ward was pretty intense at times and being fresh meat, she had to set a few doctors straight. First, she never dated doctors and second if she ever changed her mind, she'd let them all know in writing, in triplicate. That cleared the air for a while and gave her some space.

She thought to look up the Sarge, but she couldn't remember his last name. There were an awful bunch of "Sarges" in this place. During her lunch hour, she wandered through the wards, looking for a familiar name on the beds, but didn't find any.

One particularly bad day had me down at the nurses station asking for another load of Methadone. The problem was that there was nobody there that could authorize it. I was beginning to feel like I was losing it and panic started to rise up in my throat. It was just like the old times when I needed to talk to my supplier. I'd heard that another guy had taken over the job of dealing so I went and talked to him. His price was nearly double but the last thing I wanted, was to argue prices. I wanted it and I wanted it right now. All of the book learning I'd had in those classes was immediately thrown out the window.

"This is some pretty strong stuff Sarge. Are ya sure you want to do it?" he asked.

"Gimme that stuff or I'll knock your damned head off. Got that?"

He handed me a small envelope that had been folded into a square. Hard to believe that a horse would fit inside such a small barn. I already had my gear and wheeled into the furthest latrine down the hall. I was ready in just a short time and my hands were shaking badly. I missed the vein twice and then hit gold.

Damn Damn Damn. The horse bucked hard and lead me down a dead end road. The whole world was spinning and I was having a hard time breathing. Sweat was pouring from my face and I felt myself slipping out of the wheelchair. My head hit the commode as I fell, but it didn't hurt at all. Then some crazy son of a bitch turned off the lights.

When I woke up, I was on a gurney with an IV running into my arm. There was a bandage across my forehead and I felt fine, damned fine. There was a nurse taking my blood pressure and she was talking to someone across the room.

"He's having a hard time kicking the shit. He goes to the classes and every once in a while, he busts loose."

My eyes were fluttering open and closed and I heard someone say that they had known me in Viet Nam. Then I went back to sleep.

The next morning, I was awakened by an angel.

"Sarge? Sarge, can you hear me?"

I wanted to open my eyes, but bright puffy clouds were in the way, quickly rolling by like summer right after a bad storm.

"Sarge?"

I opened my eyes and stared into the brightest blue eyes I'd ever seen.

"Herman?"

Maggie laughed and grabbed hold of my hand.

"I was afraid that you weren't going to wake up. How you

feeling?"

"A little worse for wear, but I think I'll make it. When did you get here?"

"A few days ago. I looked for you a couple times. What the hell happened?"

"Well, I was having trouble with my leg and, well, it's a long story."

My head was still pretty fuzzy and in a few minutes I was back asleep. Around 1100 that morning, my Doc came in to see me.

"That was strike two Sarge. Next time you get a bad conduct discharge. Where are you getting the stuff anyway?"

I refused to burn my supplier, but in reality, he was hurting a lot of good men. The Air Police came in later in the day and questioned me about my supplier and I still refused to burn him. I saw him later that day and he had flushed all of his supplies.

I still had an IV in my arm at supper time and ate chow in bed. The food tasted like shit, but I ate anyway. I just finished my jello and Blue Eyes walked into the ward, and not even in uniform. She was wearing jeans and a sweatshirt, real civies. She sure was a beautiful woman.

"Feel like going for a ride?"

"With you, I'd go anywhere."

She laughed and it sounded like spring rain and flowers. We headed down the hall and into an elevator. Down a few floors to the main doors and outside into the afternoon sunshine. It was still pretty warm and she wheeled me into a small garden area, IV bottle and all. The place was loaded with all kinds of flowers. We took a small table and she got me some black coffee. She chose a chair right next to me and sat down. She gently placed her hand over mine.

"You know you dodged a bullet again don't you?"

"I guess I'm hooked on the stuff and I can't quit. I been using now for a couple months pretty steady."

"The next time might be the last time, even if you don't get caught. Your body can't take much more I'm afraid."

I thought about her words. Dead does last quite a while and I wasn't quite ready for it.

"Where ya from Blue Eyes?"

"Minnesota. Way up in the sticks." She smiled broadly thinking of home.

"How far?"

"How far what?"

"How far up in the sticks are you from? I'm from Minnesota too."

"Damn sure is a small world sometimes. I'm from Bear River."

"I can't believe this. I meet you half way around the world and find out you're my neighbor. I'm from Grand Lake."

Blue Eyes looked pretty surprised. We grew up only 15 miles apart and didn't even know it. I had to ask her name, but if she told me Herman again, I'd lose it for sure.

"What's your real name Herman."

"I don't usually tell anyone my name. It saves a lot of embarrassment, but for you Sarge, I'll make a trade. You tell me your name and I'll tell you mine. Deal?"

I held out my hand again and she took hold of it.

"I'm Sgt. Bill Stone. Now what's your name?"

She just sat looking at me as if she was trying to decide whether or not she wanted to really do this.

"That's a really nice name. Now remember, this is a secret. Never tell a soul. OK?"

"I promise."

She stood up and walked behind my wheelchair. Then she bent down and whispered in my ear.

"Captain Maggie Marie Moore."

The past came flooding back and I remembered the last time she was this close to me. Her perfume hadn't changed and it nearly made me fall out of my chair. I was totally overwhelmed and had a hard time thinking of what to say.

"That's a beautiful name."

"Why, thank you Sarge."

She had a smile that looked like it was aimed right at my heart. We talked until it was starting to get dark. She convinced me that I had to quit drugs and she was going to help me get through it. I'd heard them say at those classes that once you're a junkie, you're always a junkie. I was going to prove them wrong and that was that. No more drugs and when the going got rough, Maggie said that she'd be there to help me. She told me all about Methadone and how it was just more of the same.

Nobody ever kicked the habit by just switching to a different drug. I'd been through some pretty tough times in my life and quitting drugs couldn't be any worse.

The next day, I got a letter from my wife back in Minnesota. There was nothing mushy or sentimental, just the facts. She was filing for a divorce and the papers would be arriving shortly. All I had to do was sign and send them back. And then there was the little p.s. at the bottom that said, "Your Dad died.". Nothing more, just that he had died. The divorce wasn't a surprise and in some ways, it was most welcome. Dad passing away was a bit of a shock, but we were never that close anyway. He owned some property on the Bigfork River north of Grand Lake and with me being the only heir, I'd probably get it. It might be a nice place to hide out once they cut me loose from the Army.

The next morning I woke up feeling pretty good. Thoughts of my Minnesota neighbor Maggie kept me in high spirits. I ate a good breakfast and then made a call to a cousin back in Minnesota. He said that Dad had died in the hospital in Grand Lake of pneumonia. He'd been trapping beaver and tipped his canoe, dumping him into the cold river water. He lasted several days and then passed away in his sleep. He was 65 years old.

Toward lunchtime the old cravings started to come back, and I was determined not to let it get to me. I was taken off the IV once again and started back writing letters like I had before. There were so darned many wounded coming in and it seemed that they just kept getting younger. I was in demand

and it made me feel good to be thinking of someone other than myself. I dove deeper into my work and the rewards were great. Once in a while I'd run into a guy that was on a pity party, but all in all, GI's were great people.

The next evening after supper, Maggie came and got me and we went back out to the garden where we were before. We talked about everything. She encouraged me with the drug problem and renewed her contract to help me. She was an amazing woman.

"What kind of stuff did you do when you were a kid?" she asked.

"Oh I suppose it was the usual stuff a kid does. I fished and hunted and played lots of football. I lived near a lake and we spent a lot of time there fishing. Darned good place to grow up. How about you?"

"I did all the usual things in Bear River. There was cheerleaders for football and in the spring I always joined track. I just loved to run. Tell me about your family."

"There was just the two kids but my brother died when he was pretty young. Mom and Dad spent a lot of time in the bars so we pretty much raised ourselves. Then after my brother died, I started to think about things like the Army. I used to fight a lot so I figured I might just as well do it for an outfit that would pay me. I sure did like the Army, but now that's done."

"How long have you been in?"

"Pretty close to six years now. Time sure does go by fast."

"Tell me about your wife."

"Funny you should ask. Right here in my hot little pocket is the whole story. Take a look."

She took the letter from me and read it slowly.

"Kinda sounds like you're almost a single man again." she grinned.

"Yup. I suppose so. Then when I get discharged, I'll go up on the Bigfork and hide for the rest of my life. Have you ever paddled a canoe?"

"My Dad and I've paddled a million miles together. We spent a lot of time on the Big White Oak." She had a big grin on her face.

"That sure is a pretty place. My address will be close to where Hay Creek meets the Bigfork River. Just follow the your nose to the smell of frying fish. That'll be me sitting there next to the campfire at sunset."

"That sure sounds good."

We talked for quite a while and when it was time to go back in, Maggie bent down and kissed me on the cheek. I didn't even need the wheel chair. I was floating somewhere up in the clouds.

The next morning I got a message to go down to Orthopedics. The new leg had arrived and it was time for the first fitting. The stub of a leg had finally healed enough to hold a prosthesis. It looked terrible. It was a mass of hinges and junk, none of which resembled a leg. The Doctor explained everything to me. The foot was like a big spring so that it wouldn't jar my stub. He told me all of the things that I had to look out for and then proceeded to put it on me.

"I have the knee locked now so it won't dump you on the floor. After a week or so, we'll teach you how to use the knee."

I tried to stand up, but it felt strange and I sat back down.

"You're not going to get anywhere sitting in that chair. Get up slowly and grab the rails. I'll help you from there."

This time I grabbed the rails before I tried to stand and it went a bit better. I was standing, something I hadn't done in a hell of a long time.

"Now what I want you to do is lead with your new leg like you were going to take a step, but don't try to walk yet."

I pushed the new leg forward and let it drop. Then I pulled it back. I was standing and it didn't even hurt. I must have had quite a smile on my face.

"You'll make it Sarge. For now though, I want you to use a pair of crutches until you feel more comfortable."

I went to sit back down in the wheel chair and caught hell right away.

"What are you doing? Your days of wheel chairs are over and done. Now when you want to go somewhere, you long leg it, just like everyone else."

Damn it felt good to hear that. I found my way back to the ward, but I was pretty tired by the time I got to my bed. The crutches had made a bad sore spot under each arm, but I did make it, and all alone.

At 3:00 the next afternoon, Maggie walked in and asked me if I wanted to go for a ride. I said I would and stood up. She sure was surprised.

"Come on Sarge. Let's go to McDonald's."

We walked slowly out to where her car was and I got in after a little while of trying to find a place for my leg. The damned thing wouldn't bend, but I was pretty happy to be out with real people.

"How ya feeling Sarge?"

"Maggie, I think I'm going to make it."

We drove around for quite a while, Maggie making small talk and me just trying hard to absorb it all. I told her all about my neighbors back when I was a kid and she told me all about hers. By the time she dropped me off, I could almost imagine what her Dad looked like. She sure loved him.

Next week, they unlocked my knee and that was a whole new ball game. I only fell about a dozen times before I figured it out. After a while it was starting to feel more natural and I was able to lock the knee to take a step.

One afternoon Maggie and I were walking in the park, making small talk about home.

"Ya know Maggie, today's my birthday. I was starting to feel older than dirt, but you put a new spark in my life."

She reached into her purse and took out a small package tied with ribbons.

"Happy Birthday Sarge."

"Now what in the world is this and how did you know it was my birthday?"

"Well, I peeked into your chart the other day and saw it was coming up."

I opened the package and inside there was a beautiful gold set of friendship rings. They fit so closely together that you could hardly tell that there were two of them.

"Do I get one?" she asked.

I took them apart and placed one on Maggie's finger. The other was mine.

"Friends?"

"Friends." she said.

I was watching Maggie and not the ground and tripped on a small stick. Down I went, laughing and rolling down a small hill. Maggie grabbed my arm and I pulled her down to me. She put both of her hands on my face and kissed me long and gently. It was like all of the wants and wishes I'd ever known were fulfilled in just a moment of time. We stayed there for what must have been hours, just kissing and touching each other.

"I think we better go now Maggie. Another kiss like that last one and I won't be responsible for what happens next."

"If you're trying to scare me Sarge, you're going to have to work harder at it. You've still got four hours until you have to be back in the ward and I'd like to see to it that you never forget any of them."

We kissed some more and then struggled to our feet, a little worse for wear.

## Chapter: 6    Discharge

The time finally came when the Army didn't have much use for me and the feeling was mutual. It had been a long hump since I lost my leg. Maggie promised to write me, but I didn't expect to hear from her again. A good looking woman like that doesn't need a broken old sergeant to take care of.

The divorce had gone through so there wasn't any reason to go back home to Grand Lake. I spent a few days in Minneapolis and then drove up to Duluth. I spent three days just smelling the fresh air. Lake Superior was a fantastic sight. One evening I ended up in a bar on west Superior street and spent the evening watching the youngsters prove how tough they were. My days of rowdy bar fights had ended a long time ago, but still it was fun to watch. There would be a perfectly nice person walk through the door and two hours later he'd turned into a perfect asshole. In a way it was kind of funny.

I bought a brand new Ford truck and headed toward the Iron Range of Minnesota. I'd saved a lot of money over the years and now it was time to spend some of it.

# To Waltz With A White Horse

I looked for a job near Grand Lake and it seemed that they'd rather spit on me than hire me. Us "baby killers" were the scum of the earth. Finally, after several less than courteous "no thank you's" it dawned on me that there wasn't going to be a job for a one legged grunt. There was still over $10,000 in the check book so I went on the search for some kind of a business. I found a small bar up near the Bigfork River and went to the bank to discuss terms. It even had a two bedroom house next door. If I paid $5,000 down I could make the rest on payments for five years. It seemed to be about the only way I'd be able to feed myself.

The bar was a bit run down, but salvageable. There was a couple pool tables and a damned good jukebox. When I looked around, the first thing I noticed was that there wasn't an ounce of booze in the place. I'd take care of that in a hurry. I set up the joint with traps and old guns hanging on the walls and that gave it a pretty good look. I bought a few old oil lamps and hung them around for effect. There was a big fireplace and that would always be going.

I walked outside and looked around for a while. The place needed a good paint job and a sign out front. I still had to pick a name and that was getting to be a chore. It had to be something special.

I hired a couple guys to paint the place and a couple more to clean up the inside. Then I had some guys pour the footings for the new flag pole. We'd hoist old glory and keep her there as long as I was alive. I ordered a light that came on each night and kept her waving at all times. I wanted everyone to know that I'm an American and damned proud of it.

I hired a company to make me a lighted sign for outdoors and when it came down to the final name, it was either Bill's Bar or Herman's Hangout. Herman won. The day the sign came in and was installed, I opened the place for business. I'd taken care of all the licenses and permits, hired another barkeep, and sat back waiting for the money to roll in. The first week, I took in $104.00, not exactly a vast fortune. There was a catch to this, but I hadn't figured it out yet.

One afternoon an old logger walked in and asked for a shot and a snit. I figured he was an accomplished drinker by his order. By the time he'd finished a couple of those, he became pretty talkative. It seemed that I was being boycotted because I was a "baby killer". If that was the local sentiment, I'd starve to death in no time. There had to be a way to do this. I ordered a new flag, the biggest one I could buy. Then I called a guy that had left me a business card advertising his three piece band. I could afford some $100.00 music for a couple nights. Then I put a sign on the door that read, "Friday and Saturday night 5 cent beer and a damned good band". It would cost me a few kegs of beer, but it might just cut the ice.

The rest of the week saw some increase in customers, but it seemed that they just wanted to have a look around. They'd buy a bottle of beer and then play a game or two of pool, but not much conversation. The Sheriff stopped in one day and welcomed me to the neighborhood. As he finished his diet

Coke, he started to give me the rules. No selling drinks to minors. No giving away free drinks. No serving after 1:00 a.m. etc. etc. As he walked out the door, he said that he'd be watching me. If this was a subtle form of intimidation, I got the message.

Maggie was still writing to my address in Grand Lake and I wrote back once in a while. It sure would be good to see her again. It seemed that there was an empty spot in my life that only she could fill.

Whenever I'd get bent out of shape about something, the first thing that came to mind was drugs, but so far I'd been able to stay off the stuff. I was however getting to like the taste of whiskey.

One cloudy afternoon I heard a hell of a racket outside and a whole damned herd of bikers came in to get acquainted. It looked like they all rode Harley's and not a rice burner in the pack. I'd always had a good feeling about these guys and tried hard to make them feel welcome. One awful big guy came up and stuck out his hand.

"Name's Joe."

"Hiya Joe. Thanks for stopping in."

"Heard we got a baby killer running a bar here."

That one put me a bit on edge and I figured I was just going to have to show him where the bear shit in the buckwheat. I stepped from behind the bar and walked up to him. He grinned big and rolled up his sleeve. The USMC tattoo was showing proudly. Joe grinned when he saw the look on my face.

"Bet you were gonna try to whup my ass weren't ya?"

"The thought had crossed my mind."

"Every one of us were in the military and we're damned proud of it."

I walked back behind the bar and we talked for a while.

"We all been either spit on or called names." said Joe. "Nobody gets by with that any more. I'll kick ass on anybody that tries it."

Altogether the whole group numbered 23 bikers. Not a reject in the bunch.

"You gonna stick around for a while Joe?"

"We planned on it."

"Then the drinks are on me. All I gotta do is lock the door."

I went up and locked the door and made a sign that said "Private Party".

"OK assholes." said Joe. "Let's party."

The jukebox started to belt out some Rolling Stones and one of the babes in the group named Sue offered to help with the bartending. Every time I'd get too close to her, she'd pinch my ass. That woman was dead serious and by the looks of things, she could cripple a man. I'd been so busy getting the bar going, that I'd forgotten the important things in life.

I was playing pool against Joe and doing pretty darned good too. I bent over to take a shot and my knee gave out, dumping me on the floor. Joe stretched out a hand and helped me back up.

"Looks like you're not quite used to the new leg yet."

"Damned thing lets me down every time I depend on it."

"Check this out."

Joe lifted his pants leg and showed me what looked like a chunk of pipe with a boot on the end.

"This is the newest kind and it's made of titanium. The knee works great too. Won't drop you on the floor even when you're too drunk to stand up."

I asked him where he got it and he said he'd call me with the address.

That night we drank an awful lot and somewhere around 3:00 a.m. the bikers headed back home. It turned out to be one hell of nice bunch. Before they left, Joe put a coffee can on the bar and each one of them threw in at least a $20.00 bill. I was on the road to financial solvency and had made a bunch of friends too. They said they'd be back.

I locked the front door and turned off the light. The fireplace was nearly out. I took the money from the cash register and stuffed it into a bank bag. I found my way to the back door bouncing from one wall to the next, looking a bit like ricochet rabbit. I walked out the back door toward the house and looked back at the bar. The only light on in the entire area was the one that pointed up at "Old Glory" and it looked great.

I walked into the house and heard some music coming from the living room. The stereo was on and there was a light in the bedroom. I looked in and it was a candle burning in the ashtray. As my eyes adjusted to the low light level I saw the form of Sue sitting cross legged on the bed, with a big grin on her face.

She was wearing nothing but a smile. I gotta remember to lock the house when I leave.

"Hi Sarge."

Friday night came and the pace quickened some in the bar. It didn't make any difference what kind of a jerk I was, the thoughts of nickel beer were just too good to pass up. The band cranked out some of the worst music I'd ever heard, but somewhere around 9:00 it started to sound better. Jack Daniels on the rocks was my favorite poison and I tried hard to kill myself that night. It was a good thing that there was a barkeep to take care of the customers. A few of my biker buddies showed up and that had the local population looking over their shoulders. Everyone expected to see at least one gang murder, but nothing quite so dramatic took place. Everyone got along pretty well and there seemed to be a lot of laughing.

At around 1:00 the place emptied and as a few went out the door they said "Thanks Sarge". It looked like the name had followed me half way around the world.

My leg was having some difficulty holding me up. The problem wasn't the fake one. I'd drank a hell of a load of whiskey and couldn't hardly stand up. The house was only about 60 feet away, but I figured that it would be safer to park on the pool table for the night. I covered up with a jacket and that was that.

I woke up somewhere around 6:00 a.m. and was freezing to death. I felt like the entire 82$^{nd}$ Airborne had marched across my tongue. At least with drugs, I didn't feel that bad the next morning. I went into the house and brewed a pot of coffee and proceeded to make myself some breakfast. Where was Sue when I needed her! She made some damned good bacon and eggs. I'd have to settle for toast again. Some S.O.S. would be pretty fine right now.

I drove to town and stopped at the Post Office. There was a package for me and I brought it back to the truck to open it. It was a care package from Maggie. There was some homemade fudge and a ton of chocolate chip cookies. There was also a letter.

"Dear Sarge,

I haven't heard from you in quite a while so I figured that maybe you were weak and starving to death. Here's a box of goodies to help you on your road to good health. I made it all myself.

I'm going on leave soon and would like to come and see you if it would be OK. Dad is getting married to Molly in a couple weeks and I do want to be there for their big day. He sure seems to be happy.

I miss you Sarge. This nursing stuff isn't nearly as much fun without you to take care of.
Big Kisses,
Herman"

A couple weeks later, an old blue pickup pulled up to the bar with a canoe strapped on top. Some gal with an old baseball cap and worn out blue jeans walked into the bar and damned near knocked me right on the floor. Maggie had stormed back into my life. She had a grip on me and wasn't about to let go.

"Sarge, I've missed you so much."

"Maggie, it seems like it's been years. How are you?"

"I'm good. Got Dad married off and now I want to go fishing and camping for a while. Can you get away?"

"I'll lock the damned door if I have to. We'll go alright. I'll talk to my barkeep and see what he says."

Maggie was just as beautiful as the day we rolled on the ground together in Illinois. She had a smile that could kill.

"Do you remember how to cook?" I asked her.

"Never forgot. What should we have for supper?"

"Roast beef and potatoes. How does that sound?"

"Wonderful. Where's the kitchen?"

I took Maggie's bags and we headed into the house. It was in fair condition with a small amount of empty cans and TV tray junk sitting around. Living alone made me a bit of a slob.

"When do you have to go back?"

"I still have nearly three weeks."

"Can you stay here with me?"

I was serious now. This was the woman of my dreams and I didn't want to think of her ever leaving.

"I wouldn't want to be anywhere else."

She put her arms around my neck and kissed me softly, just the way she used to back in Illinois. It didn't take long and I was having thoughts that weren't at all innocent. She still had her arms around my neck and we slowly walked to the bedroom.

# To Waltz With A White Horse

Maggie cooked a fabulous dinner for us and the hired help took care of the bar. We didn't even come out for two days. It was a good thing that we had a terrific bartender to take up the slack. We talked until the wee hours each night and what was discussed sounded an awful lot like forever to me. Maggie's appetite for slow romantic sex seemed insatiable, but I did my best to keep up.

"How 'bout meeting a few of my friends tonight? Some of the bikers will be here and they're really good people."

"Sounds like a plan to me. I could use a chance to cut loose."

And with that the evening started at about 5:00. We drank a barrel of beer and danced a lot to the jukebox. The bikers were in their usual good spirits. They all liked Maggie, even if she was a "baby killer".

The next afternoon we headed over to the Bigfork River for the fishing and camping I had promised. As the sun hung brightly above the clouds, the first hint of changing colors appeared in the sumacs. While not an indicator of fall, it was still beautiful. We paddled down the river for several miles and then set up our first camp. The warm wind was blowing across the open river keeping all the bugs from draining us. Our campfire was small, but enough to fry up a couple steaks I'd brought along. Fried onions and potatoes made the meal complete. We sat on the bank of the river watching the sun sink in the west. The stars winked on one by one and soon we were trying to point out constellations. Then the northern lights started, making it seem almost magical. They would swing and sway back and forth and then start to fade only to come back brightly in another place. It was completely dark except for what the stars and the small campfire contributed.

Maggie laid back on the grass just watching the night sky.

"Do you love me Sarge?"

I was really taken aback by her question. I hadn't even thought about anything like love. It seemed to me that it didn't require saying. We had been friends and lovers for quite a while and I thought of it as being just understood.

"Of course I love you!"

There. I said it, and then I realized that I had never said that to her before. It just seemed that I didn't need to say it. She knew I loved her, didn't she?

"Are you sure?"

Hell yes I was sure. She was the one person in all the world that I felt this way about.

"Maggie, I love you more than there are stars in the sky, deeper than the deepest oceans and longer than forever. That's never going to change either."

As we sat there in the dark by the river watching the stars go by, we made a lovers pact. She was mine and I was hers. There was never going to be anything that came between us. She might be in the Army now but that would be over in a couple years.

Our canoe trip turned into a romantic interlude that would last a lifetime. We caught some fish and saw nature at its finest.

We didn't get to see Dad's cabin, but there would be time for that another day.

It was so very quiet on the river bank that night that I could almost hear "As time goes by" sung by Ella Fitzgerald. "Moonlight and love songs, never out of date, hearts full of passion" and on and on until the stars started to fade in the morning sunrise.

## Chapter: 7    The Horse Gets Loose

Maggie and I had a wonderful time together. Whenever she would go to see her Dad in Bear River it would seem that part of my soul left with her. It was a feeling of great emptiness that I couldn't start to describe. Then she would come back and the whole world would be a better place.

"I have to leave tomorrow Sarge."

"I'll hide you out and they'll never find you."

"Fat chance. I've got another two years to do and it's going to be tough without you."

"Why not just get transferred to here. I could always use a good nurse. How does Fort Herman sound?"

"Yup. That'll work." she said smiling.

We tried to cram a lot of time into the next few hours, but eventually we had to say good bye. It was hard on both of us. We made plans to see each other often with either her coming here or me driving there. When her old pickup pulled out headed south, I had a brief period where my eyes clouded up a bit. Nothing serious, but just the same I had to go in the house and take a break.

I opened the bar at noon and the regulars straggled in for their daily load of beer. Funny how it's always the same people at the same time of day and they drink the same thing and they drink the same number of bottles and say the same thing when they leave. I'd only had the place for a couple months and I was already hating it.

One morning as I headed for the bar to do some cleanup, I slipped, and the fake leg and I parted company about half way to the bar. I tried to get the leg back in the correct position, but each time I tried to pull it on, the pain nearly killed me. I'm not much of a wimp, but that day, I just couldn't do it. I crawled back into the house and called my Doc. He'd seen me before and pretty much knew my case. I had an appointment for the next afternoon.

After what seemed like a million blood tests and x-rays, he called me in to give me the good news. There was a dark spot on the x-ray that he said looked like infection. It seemed that I still wasn't done with Viet Nam. I needed more surgery and the sooner the better.

The next day I arranged to have my bartender take over while I was gone. He was a darned reliable guy and being an ex-grunt like myself, I had no problem worrying about the money. He'd take care of it as if it were his own place.

I called Maggie and gave her what I knew. It sounded like she'd be there the next day, but I convinced her that it wasn't anything to worry about.

Next morning I headed the truck south toward Minneapolis and the VA Medical Center. They seemed pretty friendly and I considered myself to be in good company. I was assigned to a ward on the fifth floor, a surgical ward. The place was humming with activity. Most of the guys there were older than me and were either from the Korean War or WWII. I got into a chariot and wheeled up to the nurses station.

"Whatcha got that I can help with? I used to write letters for the patients, but I'll take damned near anything you got."

"We do need someone to read letters and write a few too. When can you start?" the nurse asked me.

"Well, if you have some paper and envelopes, I'll start right now."

Between all of the testing, I made the rounds of the different wards. I was definitely in demand and in a couple days, it was just like being back in Viet Nam. For almost a week, I put in full days.

I got the word that I'd be having another operation on my stub. There was still a part that was infected. Depression set in and with it the old cravings for heroin. If they took much more of my stub, I wouldn't be able to wear a fake leg. The thought of that wore on me hard for the entire night and by morning, I was ready to shoot the horse. I was sweating hard and the old cravings came back in a flood.

At noon they rolled me into the operating room and the same damned angels were there wearing the same white clothes and they put the same damned Halloween mask on me as they'd done before. Ninety-nine, ninety eigh...

When I awoke, I was in the recovery room, with several nurses watching me.

"How ya feeling Sarge?"

"Wonderful!" I said, and then it was off to la la land again.

They wheeled me back up to the ward and I spent a few more days swimming laps around the inside of an IV jug. By the time I had been there for a week, the depression had a big hold on me and I was looking for a dealer. I could damned near smell them guys. It wasn't so much that you had to ask anyone, but it just became common knowledge who the dealers were. In this place it wasn't the patients that dealt the shit, it was the nurses. This time I had to go down to the third floor and look for someone named Tomisoni. I found her in the nurses lounge taking a break. All she wanted to know is how much and what kind of shit I needed. She said that she'd deliver it to me at around 11:00 that night.

By the time of the scheduled delivery, I was sweating marbles. I had stolen a syringe, a big rubber strip and found a stainless steel spoon. I was all set. The only problem was that of how pure the stuff was. Some of it was quite weak and you had to take a lot, but some of it was so damned strong that it would kill you if you weren't careful. I sprinkled some into the spoon and looked at it as if I knew what I was doing. Then I sprinkled in some more. Add the water, stir and cook. In my mind it sounded an awful lot like making chocolate chip cookies. The shit boiled and bubbled in the spoon and then

I waited for it to cool. I took the syringe out of my jammie pocket and just stared at it. The cravings were so strong at that moment that in my screwed up state, I would have killed anyone that tried to stop me. How in the hell did I get in this shape? I was sliding down a muddy hill, grabbing at small trees and grass as I slid toward the edge of the cliff.

The rubber band was wrapped around my upper arm and I made a fist to raise an artery. Yup. Right where I left it last time. I took the syringe and sucked up all the good stuff in the spoon and then I was ready. My mouth was dry and my hands were shaking. I aimed the little needle at the target and slowly pushed it into my body. Then I pulled the pin on the grenade.

I could feel it working its way into my body and I hadn't even taken off the rubber band. I set the syringe on the back of the toilet and reached up to let the horse out. It came out kicking and then in just a few seconds, I felt my heart start to jiggle like a bowl full of jello. Th th th that's all folks.

The nurse put a cold cloth on my forehead and it felt good. I was burning up inside. There was the usual IV bottle feeding into my arm.

"You have arrhythmia. Your heart wants to beat, but it's lost the rhythm. Now it just beats all over the place." said the nurse.

A doctor came in and sat down in a chair next to the bed.

"I'm Doctor Edwards. Well Sarge, you've picked a good place to die. We lose a lot of good men here every day. Some of them just die of old age, and some from battle wounds. Some die because they're too damned stupid to appreciate the life they have. I'm not a cardiac specialist, but I can tell you that if we aren't able to correct that arrhythmia, you'll be dead as hell in a few weeks."

I thought about that for a short while.

"What happened?"

"You overdosed on heroin and tried damned hard to wreck your heart. But I think that you already knew that. I have a lot of patients here that could really use my services and what's more, I think they'd appreciate it if I didn't waste my time on a loser."

With that final comment, he walked out of the ward, and I felt like shit. Because of being a weak bastard, I'd damned near killed myself.

That afternoon, they tried to get my heart back into sinus rhythm. They put the shock paddles on me and gave me a blast of electricity that made my toes curl up. They succeeded, but now it was a tossup to see if it would stay that way.

Somewhere after chow, a Chaplain came in and talked to me.

"Just stopped in to see how you're doing Sarge. I heard you're willing to sell your soul to the devil for a hit of heroin. I hope it's worth it cuz your next one will probably be the last one for you."

"I won't be doing any more drugs Padre'. I'm all done with that stuff." I told him.

He laughed a little.

"I think I may have heard that from a few other guys. Now

they're all dead."

"No. I'm serious. I got a good woman in my life and I want to spend a lot of time with her."

"I guess that whole thing is up to you, but they said that if you do it again, you're finished. If I were you son, I'd make my peace with God. I've seen this a lot of times, and you never get over the addiction."

That seemed to be the words I needed to hear. I called Maggie that night and told her what had happened. I expected to hear her say that she wouldn't be a part of this story, but all she said was that we'd whip this problem together. The tears streamed down my face and I'd have given all I own for just one hug.

I stayed in the VA hospital for a few more weeks. They made a real effort to clean up any infection that remained. We all agreed that if they took any more of my leg, I wouldn't be able to wear a prosthesis. That would be tough, but if Maggie stayed with me, I could handle it.

I spent a bit of time each day going down to the little chapel on the first floor. Just to sit there and think seemed to help. One afternoon as I sat alone, a little black woman walked in and sat by me. We talked for a while and she told me about her husband up on the fourth floor. He had been injured in Viet Nam and was having a hard time getting over it. She seemed to smile a lot and asked me what I was there for.

"I had some infection in my leg and it wouldn't heal. I think they have it under control now though."

"My man is here cuz he can't get off drugs. Every time things go a little bad, he goes back to some kind of drugs." she said.

"I got that problem too. I started to take the stuff to make the pain go away and it just kept getting worse."

The little chapel got real quiet and that little black woman started to pour her heart out, telling of all the troubles that her husband had. She never once complained of her lot in life, but she seemed so darned concerned about her husband. He was a junky, just like me and couldn't seem to get the monkey off his back.

The next day I went to see this black man with all the drug problems. He was an unusually big man with a quick smile. I parked my wheelchair right next to him and stuck out my hand.

"What's you name buddy?" I asked.

"I'm Charlie Wilson. What's yours?"

"Everybody calls me Sarge, but my real name is Bill Stone. Good to meet you Charlie. I met your wife yesterday down in the chapel. Seems like you and me got a bit in common."

The smile quickly faded from his face.

"That woman talks too much." He turned his face away, wanting me to leave.

"She seems to think that you're a pretty nice guy actually."

The smile came back and we started to talk a bit, looking around to make sure that nobody was listening in. He had about the same problem that I did. Every time things got a bit tough, we both turned to drugs. His favorite was cocaine and he was having a hard time getting off it. He'd tried the methadone route and a hell of a pile of counseling.

"What do you do for a living?" he asked.

"Well, I own a bar up north of Grand Lake, on the Bigfork River. It's called 'Herman's Hangout'. It's not too big and I got a small house right next door. Come on up and stay for a while. I'll show you where the really big fish live."

"What you in for?" he asked.

"Well, I'm having a tough time getting rid of an infection in my stub. I must have picked up a bad one in Nam. Then the damned drugs got a pretty good hold on me too. That might just be a bit harder to whip. They said that the next time I try it, I'll probably go tits up."

"Damn. I guess that's one way to quit." He grinned slightly.

"Kinda permanent though."

He told me about all of the counseling he'd been through and how the methadone was just more of the same. He said that he tried to keep a job, but the damned drugs always did a number on him. His wife worked hard just to keep food on the table. He had three kids and all were under the age of eight and that it was pretty hard on his wife.

"You know Charlie, this damned drug thing is going to kill us both. They figure that my heart can't take another dose of the stuff. I need some help getting through this."

"What do you think of teaming up with me and we help each other?"

It sounded like a pretty good idea, but I'd have to watch him every damned minute of the day. It was actually impossible. Hell, I didn't want him following me into the john just to make sure I wasn't taking drugs. There had to be a better way.

"How much time do you think you can get to go on a little trip?" I asked Charlie.

"Spose damned near as much as I want. I can't keep a job anyway."

"I got one hell of an idea. I'll tell you tomorrow what I got."

I wheeled back into my ward and got into bed. The wheels in my head were turning ninety miles an hour. If Charlie and I could go for a month without any damned drugs, we could whip this bastard. Our systems would be clear and all the bad cravings would be gone, or at least manageable. Now, how can we do this? If they would lock us each in a cell right next to each other we could do it. There had to be a way.

Next day Maggie called and we talked for a long time about making a home in Northern Minnesota after she was discharged. She promised me once more that she would stick with me and that sounded pretty good. I told her about the thing with Charlie and she said that it would work. We both had to really want it though. It sounded like we could do it.

I went to talk to Charlie that afternoon and he actually seemed glad to see me. When I brought up the part of being in a cell though, he turned cold as ice and straight out told me that he wouldn't do it. We'd have to find another way. I was heading home tomorrow to go back into the bar business up on the Bigfork.

"What do you think about coming up and doing some fishing with me? You're getting out pretty soon anyway aren't you?"

"That sure sounds like fun. I used to do a lot of paddling when I was a kid."

"What day do you get out?" I asked him.

"Actually, I get out tomorrow."

"Call your wife and tell her you're going fishing with me and you can follow me up to the river. How's that sound?"

Charlie got the biggest grin on his face. It seemed that we had a plan to go fishing.

The next day around 9:00 a.m. we started to drive north, heading for the Bigfork River Valley. The weather was pretty nice and the sun was shining brightly. We hadn't gone very far when Charlie signaled that he had to stop at the next gas station. We filled up with gas and bogey bait, just the thing for a long car trip. He still had a pretty big grin on his face each time I looked at him. The bar was still around 250 miles away, and if we kept up the same pace, we'd get there around supper time.

Next time we stopped for gas, we only had a few miles to go. We pulled into the little town of Talmoon, not far from the bar. Charlie went in to pay for his gas and when he came out he walked over to me.

"Now I might be about as green as grass, but I just gotta know who in the hell would eat leeches." he asked.

I looked at him and started to laugh.

"You better not eat them Charlie. They're fish bait."

He looked a little sheepish, but I think he was glad he didn't try any. He figured he still had a bit to learn.

The bar was as we had left it, and the whole place was loaded with them "baby killer" bikers. Sure was good to see them. My barkeep too was glad to see me. He hadn't had a day off in one hell of a long time.

"Good to see you back Sarge. See you on payday." and he walked out the door.

Guess he'd had enough of this place for a while. Charlie fit right in with the rest of the patrons and in a few minutes was telling war stories like the rest. The fact that he was a black man made absolutely no difference to any of them. He put his gear away in the house and came back in for the rest of the night. It seemed that everyone took their turn at meeting him and by closing time, he had several bottles of beer lined up on the bar. He never did get through them.

Sunday morning came and with it, a bright sky full of sunshine and promise. I had a big load of side pork frying on the stove, appropriately blackened with pepper. The coffee was pretty good too with an extra scoop to help clear the cobwebs. I heard a noise and looked up to see a great big black man clad in skivvies heading for the john. He grinned and waved as he went around the corner. When he came back out, he looked nearly human.

"What time is it?"

"I spose it's nearly 5:00 a.m. Ready to go fishing?"

"Is there any chance that there's a cup of coffee before I make that decision?" he asked.

"Hell ya. Grab a cup."

After a couple cups, he was in fine shape and ready for a days paddling on the river. I hadn't been to Dad's cabin since he passed away and I figured that today would be a good day to go. We could fish at the same time.

Charlie hadn't been kidding about knowing how to use a paddle. He was as strong as an ox and if I'd been so inclined, I think I could have water skied while he paddled. We kept a constant conversation going and both of us sure enjoyed the sights.

On that particularly sunny morning, we caught fish sometimes as fast as we could haul them over the side of the canoe. Charlie caught a northern that was way over 20 pounds and when he tried to get it into the canoe the line broke, leaving us thankful that we didn't have to share space with it.

We were still a few miles from Hay Creek and decided to paddle hard for a while to get to Dad's cabin. As we got closer, I started to get a feeling of dread. It seemed that he would be waiting for me, ready to tell me of all my shortcomings and to hand me a bucket full of advice. I had all the same old feelings that I had as a kid.

We paddled up to the cabin and pulled the canoe up on the bank a short way. We stood looking, neither of us wanting to go inside.

"Might just as well have a look." I told Charlie.

As I stepped up my foot went through the boards, sending me flying backwards off the porch.

"Now let's try this one more time." I said.

This time, we made it inside. There was no lock on the door and it came open easily. Inside it was dark and dusty. Nobody had been there since Dad died. There was still a red and white checked table cloth with a plate and a couple forks. The sugar bowl still had a few sugar cubes. He liked his coffee loaded with sugar. On the old cook stove was a pot of something that quite probably at one time was beans. Now it was hard to tell.

Charlie stood in the doorway blocking a lot of the daylight. I asked him to let a bit of light come in and he laughed. We found a lamp and chased away most of the darkness. The little cabin was actually pretty functional. There was a bed in one corner and a small cupboard. Behind the door was a steel bucket with a drinking scoop. Over near the only window was a small book stand and an assortment of books ranging from the classics to a diary. I took the diary and we left the rest of the place just as it was. We went back out near the canoe and talked for a while.

I noticed that there was a cistern pump to the south side of the cabin and walked over to see if the pump worked. I raised the handle and brought it down hard. I did this several times and nothing that looked like water came from it. I figured that the leathers were dried out. I took some river water and poured it into the top of the pump. After waiting a few minutes, I tried it once more. Each pull of the handle brought forth gushes of pure cold water, a most welcome thing on a hot day. Charlie drank until his belly sloshed with each step.

Since it was near noon, we hauled out a couple sandwiches and ate, watching the river flow by just as it had for hundreds of years. I hauled out the diary and started to look through it. In some respects it felt like an invasion of Dad's privacy. I read in the first part, about when he had gone to the Northwest Territories a long time ago. Each entry had a date. Charlie kept eating his lunch and then he started to get his stuff ready for some more fishing. I figured that we had better get moving too.

Charlie, as it turned out was a great canoeing partner and a great fisherman. Too darned bad he lived so far away. We got back to the house late that evening and went in for some supper. He did the cooking and what a good cook he was. Apparently he had paid attention when his wife made supper. He pulled out the next morning and we agreed that it had been quite a trip. He said that he'd write.

# Chapter: 8   The Plan

Maggie's job kept her pretty busy at the hospital. She saw
her share of war injuries and the disposable young men that
make a war possible. Among the most horrible of injuries were
the burn victims. There didn't seem to be any amount of pain
killer that helped them. One young doctor tried a new approach
and put a young GI into a perpetual coma feeding him with an
IV solution. He healed slowly and with each of the twice daily
changes of his dressing, they were all glad he didn't feel the
inevitable and extreme pain.

A young doctor tried to make a pass at her one day and she
felt a moment of temptation to take him up on it. She was a
young woman and felt the same urges that anyone else her age
would feel. She loved Sarge though and didn't want anything to
come between them. She thought that maybe just a short dinner
date would be fun though.

She invited him to her apartment and cooked him a nice
steak dinner. Afterwards they split a bottle of wine and sat back
enjoying the buzz and some good music. Somewhere around

9:00 he asked her to dance a slow one. That lead to some snuggling on the couch and another glass of wine. Another dance, some gentle kissing and from there it was off to the bedroom. He was a gentle lover and she felt herself drawn to him, intimately drawn to him.

Somewhere near 2:00 a.m. he headed home. Another nurse had fallen prey to his persistence. He didn't want a lasting involvement and neither did Maggie. Later that week, she found out that he was a married man. Once again she'd stepped into it. Had she known then that he was married, the evening might have turned out differently, but she wasn't sure.

She went to the orderly room and filled out a leave request for the next week, hoping to get up to Herman's Hangout and a chance to see Sarge for a few days. It was approved and she headed north on the next available flight. She arrived in Bear River and saw her Dad for a time and he laughed a bit when she said that she was going up to see Sarge for a while. He fully understood the little girl that he had raised and just told her to have a good time.

When she arrived it was nearly 10:00 p.m. on a Wednesday. She was dressed in jeans and a low cut white blouse. There were no cars around the place and no lights on in the house. She walked through the door of the tavern and Sarge looked up from his reading to see the most beautiful woman in the world. She ran to him and nearly came right across the bar at him. They laughed and kissed and laughed some more. She was going to be there for four days or more importantly four nights. She would catch up on what she had been missing and so would Sarge. The next day he called his part time barkeep and arranged for him to work the rest of the week. He now had the time to spend with her. They would go back to the place on the river she had loved so much.

Next morning their supplies were loaded and they headed upstream, paddling hard. The trip took four hours and by the time they got there, Maggie was exhausted. She fell down on the grass of the river bank and felt engulfed by her surroundings. This place was so quiet that at night you could hear your heart beating in the stillness.

Maggie and Sarge put up their tent and got the supplies taken care of. The cooler held a chunk of dry ice and that would keep the steaks frozen for quite a while. Sarge had thought to bring some wine, but had changed his mind. Maggie put a minnow onto a hook and cast it out into the current to rest on the bottom. She sat watching the line but nothing happened so she laid back on the grass and watched the bright puffy clouds of summer float by headed for somewhere. Thoughts ran through her head and she replayed the night, not too long ago when the new doctor came to dinner. She felt a little guilty about it, but damn, it sure felt good. Now she thought of what might be ahead once again tonight. She was developing a taste for hard sex and hoped that it wouldn't make Sarge wonder where it came from.

Her fishing line was wrapped around her foot and it gave a hard jerk. A fish was on the line and she better get serious or lose it. She stood up and started to fight the fish with Sarge cheering her on. Then the line went slack and she lost it, cut most likely by the teeth of a small northern.

He came to sit by her in the sun and it turned into a round of lovemaking that took him by surprise. She lead him through all the pits, mountains and minefields, over the edge of a cliff and dropped him back once again on the bank of the Bigfork River, safe and sound. He felt like he had been put on heavy duty wash and spin dry. As he sat on the river bank she stood naked in front of him, sparkling with perspiration. She lifted up her bra to him.

"Think I need this?"

"Damn Maggie. You could be arrested for attempted murder. I was starting to think my heart would just up and quit."

"You better get used to it big boy." and she stepped a bit closer to him.

There would be no good that could come from telling Sarge about her night with the doctor. She'd keep it to herself and try to keep it to an absolute minimum, if ever again.

Supper time came and it was decided by unanimous vote that Maggie would cook. She had packed a pair of large steaks and a few onions. She started the onions going in a big cast iron frying pan. When they were nearly browned, she opened two cans of mushrooms and threw them in too. As they sizzled, Sarge was feeling his taste buds awaken. She poured them onto a plate and put the steaks on to cook. While they were browning, she threw a pair of potatoes into the coals and that was the final ingredient.

A few minutes later she heard one of the potatoes pop and that was the signal. She took them from the coals and brushed them off. She set each one on a plate and opened them up for the butter. Then she produced a bit of sour cream and a jar of horseradish, the sour cream was for the spuds and the horseradish was for Sarge and him alone. Then came the steaks. She placed them on the blue steel plates and covered them up with onions and mushrooms. She handed the first one to Sarge and then sat down next to him with hers. It was extremely evident that she had done this before.

That evening as we sat on the bank of the river, I started to tell Maggie what I had found in the old cabin. The diary was written as if Dad was talking to me directly.

"Tell me what it had to say." said Maggie.

"Well, some of it is kinda personal, and some was a bit hard to understand. I guess the main part is that Dad left me the directions to a real, honest to goodness, gold mine. I mean a real, money in the bank, gold mine."

"Let's go and look at it."

"Well Babe, you better get in shape first. It's probably over a thousand miles from here and all by river. The directions tell of each landmark along the way, but doesn't actually say where it is. Another funny thing is that he left me a sack of gold nuggets but I can't remember where it is."

"You have to be kidding."

"No kidding here at all. He said that it was buried a foot

deep under the rock I sat on when I shot my first duck. I'll be damned if I can remember where that is."

"Sounds to me like you better start doing some heavy duty remembering." said Maggie.

"I sure have been trying, but I was only about 7 years old."

"Bill Stone. Is this for real or did I work you too hard in the sun?"

"Maggie, I think it's for real. Dad got old and just couldn't make the trip back to get to the gold. He left me the directions of how to get there, but even that was in the form of a puzzle."

"Did you find it?" she asked.

"Yup. Right where he said it was. It was in an old mason jar."

"This is just too impossible. That stuff never happens for real."

"Well Maggie, this time it is for real. My Dad was no bullshit'er. He never joked around, always dead serious. Now listen Maggie. This is going to be one hell of a trip."

"How long do you think it will take?"

"I would guess that it would take around 3 months for the whole thing. Might be a lot longer than that."

"That leaves me out."

"I kinda figured that. But there is a guy that I met in the VA hospital. He's a junkie like me. We talked about getting locked in a cell for a month to get the drugs out of our systems and give us a new start. This would be just as effective and might make a new man out of each of us."

"Sorry Sarge. There's no way I can let you be gone for that long." and she laughed.

"I'd sure miss you Maggie, but the way I feel is that this might be my last chance to get off the drugs. They said that the next time, might just kill me. I sure don't want that."

Maggie hung her head a bit looking at the ground between her feet.

"I guess there is something to that, but I still would miss you."

"From all I've been able to find, the whole trip would be remote with little or no chance to communicate back here to the states."

The rest of the trip was about as good as it gets. They fished, made love, ate, made love and then when there was a free moment, Maggie would tackle the poor old Sarge for some more. They acted a lot like school kids in love, and felt like it as well. When they finally came back to the bar, Maggie was already running behind time and had to leave for Illinois. They held each other for a long time and promised to be faithful to each other.

"Charlie? This is Sarge. How the hell are ya?"

"Well, I been tryin' to stay clean, but it's been hard."

"I hear ya. It feels like I'm only an inch away from the needle all the time."

"Me too."

"Listen Charlie. Something came up that you might be interested in."

Charlie and I talked for quite a while and he really seemed interested. The idea of going remote for three months would clean us out for sure, and I told him we'd split anything we find 50-50. That sparked his interest for sure. His wife wouldn't have to work so hard trying to feed their family.

Saturday morning as I sat eating my breakfast in the quiet of the little house, it came to me where I shot my first duck. It was right where the Salem creek enters the Bigfork River. I could almost see it from the breakfast table. Dad had me set up with a 20 gauge shotgun and we had put out a couple dozen mallard decoys. The sun was just starting to lighten the fall sky and a huge flock of greenheads came in on us. Dad gave me first shot.

There was still another three hours until I had to open the bar to the local population but it was probably enough to get to the duck blind and back again. I found a spade in the shed and threw it into the truck.

I turned in at the nearly hidden narrow road that lead to the river and started looking for anything that was familiar. I almost drove right into the water. Apparently this was a spot that people used quite often to fish from the river bank. I looked around for a while and saw the small point of land where the creek and the river came together. It sure had been a long time and a pile of miles since I'd been here last. I walked into the woods a short way and found some dry ground that lead in that direction. The smells of the river and the sounds of all those birds brought me back to a time so very long ago when Dad and I were actually friends. It really wasn't for a long time, but still there was a time.

Eventually I came to the place I was looking for and in the mosquito infested swamp, I found the very rock that I used to sit on. There was just for a moment, the same smells of the rice paddies in Viet Nam and it sent chills down my back.

The damned bugs were trying their best to carry me away. I put the spade under the edge of the rock and tipped it over and out of the way. I took a spade full of dirt, looked it over thoroughly, and threw it into the river, then another and then another. The hole was nearly as deep as I thought it should be and with the next scoop, I uncovered a small leather pouch, mostly` rotted away with small pieces of gold mixed in with the mud. My heart did a flip flop and I realized at that moment that maybe this wasn't all just a joke after all. The gold was no more than a big handful of pretty rocks, and not so much that it wouldn't fit into one pocket. I made sure that I had it all and headed back to the truck and home. The drive home gave me a bit of time to sort it all out. If this was indeed a trail to a gold mine, I was ready.

A plastic bucket would work well and I filled it with warm water. I remembered from my days at the movies that gold sinks to the bottom so I stirred it all up vigorously and poured out the muddy stuff. Then I did it again and kept at it until the water ran clear. I lifted the bucket and poured the rest of the water out onto the gravel driveway. There in the bottom of the bucket was a big handful of the prettiest gold any man had ever seen. I could feel my pulse quicken and my forehead start to sweat.

I took it into the house and poured it out onto the kitchen counter. I think the appropriate word is yourika or myeka or somebody's eeka. I sat down on the stool and looked it over closely. Maybe it was fools gold, pyrite. No. Dad was far to smart for that and he'd never do that to me. Damn. This had to be gold.

I spent a rather long day and an even longer night waiting until it started to get light so I could head to Grand Lake and a jeweler. They had ways of testing gold.

The test came back to be nothing less than pure gold. At $18.00 an ounce the man offered me nearly $200.00 for it all. No sale.

"Charlie. You won't believe this."

"Wait a minute. Who is this?"

"Dammit Charlie. It's me Sarge."

"What's on your mind? Sounds to me like you're about to have a heart attack."

"I found that gold sample and it came out to be 100% pure. Charlie, we're heading north."

"Are ya sure Sarge? That's a long time to be gone from home, but I ain't no damned good to anyone here. When we leavin'?"

With that, the plan was made. We'd need a hell of a pile of very specific supplies and one damned good canoe. I figured if we took dehydrated food and water purification tablets we'd have a good start on what we'd need.

Charlie came up for a day near the weekend and we went through everything we'd need. He had been trained in survival and so had I. We both knew navigation and were good with a paddle. Aside from having a fake leg, I figured that I could do it without any trouble.

The plan was for us to leave on Wednesday morning at sunrise. Charlie said that he'd be here the day before. I called Maggie and told her the plan. She sounded excited, but I don't think she wanted me to be gone for so long. Maybe that was just a bit of wishful thinking.

Tuesday night Charlie and his wife and a load of kids drove into the yard and I got big hug from that nice little woman I had met in the chapel. She dressed me down, telling me to watch out for her husband and then gave me a big grin. She put her arms half way around Charlie and hugged him hard. So did the kids. They sure looked small standing next to him. He took each child in turn and scooped them up into his big arms. Each one was told to look out for their Mother and each other and kissed severely.

"Bye Papa." they all yelled as they left.

I looked over at Charlie and that big ape had a pretty sad look on his face. He sure seemed to have a big heart.

That night I called Maggie again to say good bye and we talked for quite a while. She sure didn't want me to go, but it was a good plan no matter how it turned out. The bar business was taken care of with a darned good man that I could trust.

That took some of the pressure off me.

Sunrise was still an hour away and I was loading the truck. The barkeep would pick it up later on. By the time Charlie woke up, it was nearly light. That would be the last time in quite a while he would get to sleep in so late. We ate some bacon and eggs and headed out, not quite knowing what we were up against. If there was anyone in the world I'd rather share a canoe with, it would have to be Maggie, and that's the only one. Charlie was no slouch at paddling if I could keep him from pulling too hard and breaking the paddles. Our plan was to have him in front, since he had better eyes than me and seemed to have no trouble reading the water and the rapids.

We set the canoe into the water. It barely weighed 60 pounds and cost a small fortune. The guy I bought it from said that you could wrap it around a tree and it would straighten back out again. I didn't figure to test it. Then came the two pack frames and a rucksack full of food. After that, came the tools that we'd need to get the gold out of the ground. I had the maps and directions duplicated and covered with plastic, just in case we went for a swim. That and three extra paddles, made up the entire load. It seemed that we should be able to portage in one trip.

I looked over my shoulder to the east and the sun was just poking it's head over the cat tails. I felt a bit apprehensive right at that moment. Here we were, about to take on an adventure the likes of which few had ever seen. In some ways it was like stepping into the mouth of the dragon, unsure if he had just eaten or not. Once we dipped the paddle into the river and took that first bite into the current, we would be committed and nothing would make us turn back. If it came to a hard spot, there would be no drugs to fall back on. This indeed was a trip designed to change lives.

Charlie stepped in and settled his big frame down in the canvas seat. Then he looked back at me with a most serious look on his face.

"What do ya think Sarge?"

"Lock n load."

The trip had begun.

## Chapter: 9   Combat Wounded

Somewhere near the end of the first week that they were gone, Maggie started to have thoughts of things like drownings and accidents. In her heart she knew how capable that pair of adventurers were, but still it was the uncertainty that got to her. Her work kept most of her time occupied.

The Viet Nam war was still going strong and Mr. Kissinger was making many trips to Paris in an attempt to come up with a final solution. The daily network news reports always contained the inflated body counts, but still the American casualty numbers rose each week.

Jane Fonda got her picture taken in Hanoi, while climbing onto an enemy artillery piece. Not more than a mile away from that fiasco, damned good American troops were being beaten, tortured, and humiliated in unspeakable ways. Some people wondered out loud, whether or not their son would have been killed if she had stayed home. Uncle Ho Chi Minh was having a field day seeing her betray her own people.

That little public relations show by Fonda gave courage,

aid, and comfort to the enemy and Maggie had the opportunity to see the results first hand. The numbers of wounded grew each day and they were ordered to work six 12 hour shifts per week and asked to volunteer extra hours whenever possible. Even the local community of civilians came in to help out wherever they could.

Maggie made a new friend in her ward, another nurse from Minnesota. They spent a lot of time talking about high school and their teachers. Her name was Sarah and she was from Minneapolis. They talked about family and that seemed to reduce the stress that each of them felt from their jobs.

One evening she called Maggie to see if she wanted to go on a double date. She declined saying that she was in love with Sarge and didn't want to do anything that might wreck their relationship. After she hung up, she thought of how good it felt to stay faithful to her man. She would remain this way, hoping for his early return.

Sarge and Charlie crossed into Canada in under a week and the paddling was getting to be a bit more difficult. They were moving along keeping a good rhythm and suddenly they were in a stretch of rapids that looked like it might go on forever. The noise of the water churning all around them was nearly deafening. Charlie should have seen it and warned Sarge, but they were now in the middle of it and no where to go but down stream. All their senses were on high alert and they paddled hard, trying their best to stay away from the boulders and tree stumps. There was a small spot of calm and then it was right back into the jaw of the beast. Just for a moment, Charlie looked back at Sarge.

"Are we having fun yet?" he asked yelling at the top of his voice.

Sarge splashed him with his paddle. It seemed to defuse the situation for a bit, but they still had a hard stretch to go. Then it came to him that this was what had been lacking in his life. Challenge, the kind that if you make the wrong choice, you die. This was what got his heart in high gear. This was his heroin, his horse.

The river went back to fairly smooth, but his heart was still beating hard asking for more heroin. It had been the every day life threatening challenges that he needed. His time in Viet Nam was what had made him an addict to danger.

They found a granite outcrop that looked like a great spot to spend the night and pulled in as soon as they could.

"What the hell is that grin about?" asked Charlie.

"Oh nothing much. I love to run those rapids. It gets this tired old heart beating and it sure feels good."

"I know what you mean. That's the first time in years that I really felt in danger and it felt damned good."

His voice was filled with excitement.

"Good thing I didn't take Maggie on this trip. I doubt that she could have done it."

"My muscles were sore for the first few days, but now I'm back to fighting form." he laughed.

Sarge found a comfortable spot to sit and took out his journal. He wrote in it each day.

"Do you always keep a diary?"

"I used to a long time ago, like my Dad, but not for quite a while."

"What do you write in that thing?"

"Oh, it's just about the day, the weather, the river and mostly what I see and feel." said Sarge.

"I never tried that, but it sounds like something I'd like to do."

Journal: Wednesday July 23rd

It turns out that Charlie is an excellent person to have on a trip like this. Maggie is in my thoughts most of the time. The rivers have been tough but it feels good to test myself. This is going to be a long trip and heroin is on my mind like a thorn in my side. A bottle of whiskey would even taste good. Charlie seems to have his addiction whipped.

End

They sat watching the sun go down and the river had turned calm. They were far from the noise of the rapids so each bird and frog sound seemed to be amplified and loud. Darkness settled on them slowly and Sarge walked uphill a short way to a spot overlooking the river. He sat down and looked around. This was the most beautiful place he'd ever seen. All that was missing was Maggie.

As he sat there watching and listening, darkness settled around him. There were no stars because of the cloud cover, so when it was dark, it was very dark. His Dad used to say it was blacker than the inside of a cow. The darkness covered him like a black velvet blanket making him feel secure. His thoughts wandered for a time back to when he was just a kid. His Dad had a bad problem with alcohol. He spent nearly all the family money on booze and when it came time for new clothes, there was no money. He had to mow lawns and do a lot of chores to get enough for school clothes. He thought that maybe his father had given him this gold mine to make up for all the bad days. He hoped so.

As he sat in the stillness, he tried to remember his feelings the first time he saw Maggie. It could have been in the operating room or maybe the recovery room. Her blue eyes seemed to be nearly hypnotic. When she spoke, it gave him the feeling that she was talking directly to his heart. He closed his eyes, but it made no difference. The blackness was deep and endless.

When it was time to go back to the fire, he had to use a flashlight to find his way.

"I thought you left and went back home." said Charlie.

"No. Just gathering my thoughts. How did you ever get hooked on drugs anyway?"

"I think that I've been a junkie since I was just a kid. All of us in the neighborhood used anything we could either smoke, sniff or just stuff up our noses. I can't remember a time when I didn't use one thing or another."

"Sounds like a tough way to grow up."

"It was. Another part is the fact that way over half the kids I grew up with are dead now. Most of them from overdose, but a few shot too. Damned tough life for all of us."

"Where did you live?"

"We lived in Denver, near Colfax Avenue. During the day it looked nice and clean, but as soon as it got dark, the rats came out to look around. When I was about nine, my best friends were prostitutes. They used to kinda look out for me.

When I got to be 15, I had a job at the Crazy Horse bar, pimping for a gal I knew. Every night, she'd either give me money or drugs.

We had hard times too, times when there just wasn't any food in the house. Then my Mama would go and sell herself on the street, bringing a strange man back to the house. We learned early to stay in our room until we heard them leave. I had a sister a couple years younger than me and I always tried to take care of her. She'd cry when she heard the new man come into the house."

"Don't think I could handle that."

"You'd be surprised at what you can handle when you have to. Mama had a boyfriend that moved in with us for a while. Every time that she'd leave, that bastard would try to screw my sister. She was so damned scared of him that she'd stay in her room hour after hour just so she didn't have to see him. I was 16 then and I warned him to leave her alone. He slapped me hard and knocked me on the floor.

The next afternoon when I came home, Sis was crying and I

knew what had happened."

"What'd you do?"

"Now listen Sarge, you can't tell a soul. Understand?"

In the flickering firelight, Sarge saw a large man, just a man, that was about to bare his darkest secrets to a good friend.

"Sure."

"Well, that night I saw him standing outside the Crazy Horse bar. He looked over and saw me. He straightened up some and walked toward me. I ducked around the corner into the shadows and walked to the back of the building, slow enough so he'd follow me. Then I stopped and put my hand on the knife I had in my belt. I looked around to see if anyone was watching. He put his hand on my shoulder and I spun around and stuck the knife in his belly. His eyes opened wide and it looked like he was trying to talk. He still had his hand on my shoulder and I just kept my hand on the knife. Slowly he sunk to the ground, still trying to talk.

We never had any more trouble with him. In a couple days, I went through his suitcase to maybe learn a little more about him. There was a couple pictures of different women and one of a young kid.

My mother asked if we'd seen him around and I just said no. There was never any police knocking on the door either. I hated that bastard for what he'd done to my sister and mother and I think if I had to do it again, I could."

"Sounds like you grew up whether you wanted to or not."

"Sure did."

# To Waltz With A White Horse

"We had tough times too. One winter we lived out in the woods in a one room cabin with a barrel stove for heat and cooking. The food was gone and one morning when I woke up, there was nothing at all to eat. I mean there wasn't enough food in that place to keep a mouse from starving.

It was getting near to spring time and the snow was starting to settle some. I didn't have a gun so hunting was out of the question. It was about 30 degrees outside so I put my coat on and went looking for something to eat. I'd only walked about a mile down the highway when I saw a dead skunk right in the middle of the road. It didn't stink too bad. I walked on past it and then thought that it might just be something we could cook. I walked back and picked it up. I carried it home and skinned it out. The meat was dark red and wasn't in too bad of shape. I took it inside and we cooked it in a pan on the stove."

"You mean to say, you ate that thing.?"

"Damned sure did. I don't know if you've been really hungry before, but it's something you never forget. Even to this day, I buy way more groceries than any man could use. Guess I just don't want to run out."

"Guess you've had some hard times too." said Charlie.

"Guess we both have. Just look at us! A couple old junkies trying to make it through another day."

"I guess you could say that, but we're alive and not quite ready to give up yet."

Charlie got up and put a couple more pieces of wood on the fire. The stars were bright and an owl said hello from a tree nearby. Their camp on the river remained quiet for the rest of the night, both men digesting all they'd heard.

The next day found them again in some hard rapids and a small waterfall made a portage an absolute necessity. That took them the better part of three hours to get around. The trip was starting to wear on them both. According to all of the directions that his Dad had left him, it seemed that they still had a very long way to travel. Sarge had brought some good maps and kept close track on where they were.

One evening they sat watching the fire and they both looked up when they heard a train whistle in the distance. Each of them pointed to where they thought the sound came from and then went to the map. They set the map on the ground oriented to the north and drew a line to where they thought the train was.

"This is where I think we are, and according to that train whistle, we're right here."

He pointed on the map.

"Hell. We're only a few miles from Madera. Wanna go have a beer?"

"No. I think we better stick to business. This is a hard trip and we need to make time." said Sarge.

"You're right. If anyone knew what we were doing, we'd have quite a following."

That evening before dark, Charlie walked up on the ridge behind them and stayed gone for a while. When he came back, Sarge saw that Charlie was a bit more talkative and there was some white powder under his nose. Sarge just watched for a while until he was sure.

"You son of a bitch. You brought your drugs with didn't you."

Immediately, the expression on Charlie's face changed to one of unbridled rage. He'd been found out and now it was in the open. Then just as fast as it came, his face mellowed some and became somewhat softer.

Sarge drew himself up to his full height and spoke with authority. For a moment it was as if he were back in charge of his troops.

"What in the hell are you talking about?" said Charlie.

"You know damned good and well what I mean. You brought some cocaine with you. Tell me the truth you bastard or I'll leave you right here in the damned woods."

Charlie hung his head and wouldn't say anything. Sarge stood tall, looming tall over the junkie.

"Go and get the shit and do it now."

Charlie reached over and pulled his ruck sack to him. He pulled out two small plastic sacks of cocaine and handed them to Sarge.

Sarge took the bags and held them close to the fire to examine them. Here was what he'd been craving for the last several weeks, but if he gave in to the shit, he'd quite possibly never make it back home and what was even worse was that if he did get back, he'd still be a junky. He opened the bags and with Charlie watching, sprinkled the white powder into the fire. The flames consumed the cocaine and Charlie cried like a baby. Sarge too was a bit shaken, but his training made him take charge and that was what he did.

They broke camp at around 5:00 the next morning. Charlie did his work, but refused to make eye contact with Sarge. It was either from anger or possibly that he was so ashamed that he had bowed his head to the "master", cocaine. Addiction did different things to different people. Some got real quiet when they needed a hit. Some got boisterous. Some fell deeply into the pit of depression. That's where Charlie was, about 25 feet below the level ground and reaching for air. He was sinking and Sarge had just thrown him a rope.

Charlie was a big man and if so inclined could break Sarge in half, but he was a gentle man too and the monkey had taken up residence on his back. On this day they were both pretty quiet and paddled hard, eating up the miles. The sun was beating hard on their backs and Charlie's muscles rippled hard with each pull.

"How ya doin' today?" asked Sarge speaking loudly so he could be heard over the noise of the river.

"I'm OK. I been thinking about that damned cocaine. I came with you to dry out, but was so stupid that I brought the shit with me. I'm really sorry Sarge."

"No big thing Charlie. I think that if we work together we can whip this thing."

"God I sure hope so. Even today, I feel such a craving for more."

The two pretty much made a brand new agreement that neither of them would ever do any more drugs.

Back in the hospital in Illinois, Maggie was working double shifts and it was wearing hard on her. She looked in the mirror and saw the beginnings of stress lines in her face. It scared her some. She went to the gym and worked out for a while trying to relieve some of her anxiety. It helped a little, but she sure missed Sarge. The bad part was not knowing where he was or how he was. That trip was a long one for a couple junkies.

Maggie was promoted again and that brought her monthly pay up to where she could get a different apartment off base. Her and a few friends got the move done in two days. The new place had a swimming pool and she took advantage of it whenever she could.

On one quiet Sunday morning, she was near the pool, wearing her swim suit. The sun was hot and she was doing her best to get a tan. A man walked up to her and asked for directions to a certain apartment number.

She said that it was near hers and she was just going to go inside. As they walked along, Maggie was starting to get a bad feeling about this guy. They got near her apartment and she said that it was just the next place. She found her key and he walked toward the next door. As soon as she got the door open, he rushed her and pushed her inside. She tried to scream, but he hit her hard across the face, knocking one of her front teeth out. She fell to the floor and he dragged her into the bedroom. She was conscious at that point, but barely. He ripped her clothing to shreds and left her sobbing in fear.

The next few minutes passed with this grunting pig raping her. He must have felt it was pretty good, but she felt nothing but revulsion. She memorized everything about is face, down to the smallest details. His clothes, his stinking smell of grease and oil, his hair, were all memorized.

When he got done with his rape, he dressed again and walked out of her bedroom and into the kitchen. He had the audacity to even make himself a sandwich. She was extremely afraid that he would kidnap her but in just a few minutes, he came back into her bedroom and made a comment about how good she looked. Then the phone rang and he ran out into the hallway and was gone.

She made her way to the bathroom and scrubbed herself from top to bottom several times trying desperately to remove any trace of the rapist. He had degraded her and left her with a beaten and swollen face. She sobbed uncontrollably for quite some time and then called her closest friend Sarah. She came over right away and found Maggie with her face bruised and her front tooth broken off. They both cried for a while and then Maggie started to get mad. She called the police and they sent two detectives over to take her statement. Then she called her commanding officer. He gave her three days off and made an emergency appointment at the base hospital and the dentist. She needed two stitches in her lip.

After the three days were up, she still looked like hell and called the commanding officer. He told her a few options and gave her the rest of the leave she had saved up. That gave her another three weeks to heal.

The detectives called her at home one morning and asked if she would mind looking at some mug shots. She drove in and picked out her assailant in just a few minutes. Manny Rodriguez, a small time criminal and shakedown artist was the bastard who had raped her.

The next day she went down and picked him out from a lineup. She had his face burned into her memory and nothing was going to change that. She missed Sarge really bad, but the thought of telling him that she'd been raped was worrying her. He might not want her any longer and that would just kill her.

The trial came up in a short time. The evidence was overwhelming and his fingerprints placed him at the scene. He plead guilty and was sentenced to 15 years in prison. The Judge made the sentence as stiff as possible with no chance for parole or early release.

Maggie applied for an early discharge from the Army and resigned her commission. Her last day was at the end of her leave. The dentist had made her a partial for the missing tooth and she was nearly back to the way she used to look. Deep inside though, she still carried a lot of hatred around.

A few friends met at a local bar to give her a send-off and she drank a single drink. She felt a drastic need to be in complete control and if she weakened even for a second, her whole world would go flying apart. These people had been her supporters through the entire ordeal and tomorrow she would get into her car and drive slowly to Minnesota. There were lots of tears and laughter.

The day dawned bright and sunny. She put the last of her clothes into a brown paper bag and threw it into the trunk. The engine came to life and she started her trip to Bear River, Minnesota, a long way down the road.

At noon on her second day out, she arrived in Grand Lake and picked up a few groceries to take to her Dad's house. He and Molly would be glad to see her and insist that she stay there with them. Her plan was to go up to Herman's Hangout and help run it while Sarge was gone. They hadn't discussed it at all of course, but she was pretty sure he'd like the idea.

Sarge and Charlie had been on the river trail for weeks and were starting to feel a bit wore down. The river took them under a bridge and being real quiet, they could hear what sounded like a town close by. They pulled up on the river bank and climbed the hill near the bridge. There not more than one block away was what looked like a very small town. They went back and covered the canoe with grass and branches.

"What do you think about a real meal that doesn't smell like wood smoke?" asked Sarge.

"I'm so darned hungry I could eat a cow, hide and all."

"Let's go have a look."

There was a small restaurant and a gas station. Across the road was a small bar. They chose the restaurant and walked in. By the looks they got, it appeared as if they didn't get many visitors.

"I didn't hear you drive up. What can I get for you boys aye?"

"The first thing I want is a cold glass of milk." said Charlie.

"Make that two." said Sarge.

The waitress brought them their milk and a couple menus and then gave them a few minutes to read it over.

"What you gonna have Sarge?"

"I think I'm gonna have a big steak and a baked potato and another glass of milk. How 'bout you?"

"To tell you the truth, I'm really hungry for a good breakfast."

"What can I get you boys?" asked the waitress.

The little restaurant had only four green tables and a small counter. Everything looked clean, but well worn.

They ate like they hadn't been fed in quite a while and felt like new men filled up with good food and enthusiasm. They walked across the road to the grocery store and stocked up on a few things they needed, then walked back to the canoe and uncovered it.

"I sure feel a lot more like paddling Sarge."

"Ya. Me too. We should look over the maps before we head out again. That might give us a good idea of how much further we have to go."

The results of the map study revealed that they probably still had a lot of paddling left to do. The directions were extremely vague. First you go to this rock and then to the next rapids with the big pine trees and so on. You just never knew what your destination was from the directions. They just had to keep paddling, one landmark at a time. According to the map, they had crossed into several different rivers and had a lot more to go.

Charlie was getting a bit agitated one evening, needing a hit of cocaine. As they sat near the fire Sarge could see that Charlie's hands were shaking a bit and he kept staring off into the distance. He was in a bad way and there wasn't anything that either of them could do to help. It was almost 11:00 p.m.

"Let's load her up Charlie. We need to make some time and with a full moon, we shouldn't get into too much trouble."

"You're nuts Sarge!"

Sarge started to load up the canoe and poured some water on the fire. By that time Charlie had it figured that Sarge had a screw loose, but he'd go along just for the hell of it. Sarge got into the canoe and waited for Charlie.

"You coming along?"

"Sarge. You're a hard case."

"Harder than you'll ever know you big shithead."

Charlie got in and they started to paddle. Sarge was intent on making good time and Charlie had to keep up or die trying.

"Are you nuts? Damn. Slow down a bit." said Charlie. But Sarge just poured the coal on and paddled even harder. This continued in the darkness for nearly three hours. Then they came to a stretch of rapids that they didn't think should be tried until it got light.

"What do you think Charlie? Should we wait a bit?"

"I'm about beat Sarge."

They beached the canoe and Charlie fell out onto the ground.

"Need any cocaine?"

"What?"

"You need a fix?" asked Sarge.

Then it came to Charlie what had happened. Sarge saw him in one of his worst moments and risked his life to help him. Paddling an unknown river in the middle of the night was nearly like putting a gun to your head, but it took the miserable cravings from him. Back at the last campsite, he had felt like he would go insane in just a short while. Sarge saved his life and he wouldn't forget it.

They slept for a while and then got up to make a pot of coffee. Sarge had it all under control with the pot bubbling away making a loud hissing sound with each drop wasted in the fire.

"You saved my butt Sarge. Thanks."

"I'd like to take credit for it Charlie, but last night I was in just as bad a shape as you were. If we wouldn't have hit the river right then and there, I would have had a damned tough time myself. See Charlie, we help each other."

Charlie grinned.

"Coffee?"

"Sure." said the big black man.

They were really starting to become close friends. Sarge was spending a lot more time writing in his journal. He figured that if he didn't make it, someone would at least find the gold. He had somewhat revamped his plan. Wherever his Dad's directions took them, they would find the gold and then look for a way out. There was no chance at all of paddling a canoe upstream all the way back to Minnesota. Charlie was willing to give it a try, and Sarge respected him for it.

That evening Sarge went to sit by the river. He found a nice soft spot and just sat looking around. His thoughts wandered for quite a while from one thing to another and then settled on a time when he was in Viet Nam.

He was on guard duty during a time that the Viet Cong were using kids to kill the Americans. Earlier in the week he had seen a small girl pull the pin on a grenade and hand it to a GI. They were both killed. This stuck in his mind like a living breathing nightmare.

A young boy no more than six walked toward him and he raised his gun telling him to stop. The little one just kept coming with his hand outstretched. He was carrying something brown a little bigger than his hand. When he got within twenty feet, he still wasn't sure so he capped the kid right in the head. He fell to the ground kicking his feet back and forth in the dusty road. Sarge walked up to him and saw that he had been carrying a candy bar. He had wanted Sarge to buy it from him.

He'd only been in country for a couple months and so far he had stayed alive by being careful, but today all that went down the drain. He'd killed a kid, a small kid. His commanding officer knew what had happened and didn't take any disciplinary action. He didn't need to. Sarge felt strong remorse for a long time. No matter what he did, he couldn't get the kid's face out of his thoughts.

He moved back to the fire.

The next day as they paddled along, they were looking for a landmark that meant they were on the right track. It was an overhanging shelf of granite with two large boulders close to the water. Near dark, Charlie found the place they had been looking for. Then they knew that they were still on course.

They quickly built a fire and Sarge read out of his Dad's journal.

"If you get this far, you're doing well. There's still a weeks paddling to do. Throw a line into the river just off the smaller rock."

"Wonder what that's all about." said Sarge.

Charlie already had his rod and reel set to do some fishing. He cast out the small lure and immediately a nice fish grabbed it. He pulled in a nice walleye and then another and another. Sarge didn't even have time to fish, he was too busy cleaning what Charlie caught. He stopped fishing at four and got ready for a nice meal of the world's finest fish.

"I guess I was starting to wonder what we'd have for supper, but you sure fixed that problem." said Sarge.

## Chapter: 10    Bad River

Sarge had read and reread his Dad's journal and directions many times. Some evenings, he'd just sit and try to understand what he could have been thinking and feeling as he wrote. One part was an extreme mystery to him. It read as follows:

"Watch out while you're in the "Bad River" area. This is an old Indian burial place and the general area goes on for many miles. I saw some things that just plain scared me to death. There was a raven that stayed near me for the entire time I was there."

He showed it to Charlie and they both got a laugh out of it. No damned bird was going to run them off or make them turn back.

An afternoon of hard paddling sent them to the river bank early one day. They were both tired out and needed to catch up on their rest. Sarge had a fire going and Charlie was peeling a couple potatoes to go along with a fish that he'd caught. It looked like it was going to rain so they took out their tent and set it up near a high spot a short way from the river bank. Sarge went and tied the canoe to a tree just in case the river rose during the night.

Not much was said for quite a while.

"How long has that raven been sitting there?" asked Sarge.

"What raven?"

He turned his head to where Sarge was looking. Not far away, a large raven sat quietly on the branch of a large cedar tree, just watching them.

"Guess I hadn't noticed."

The large black bird just sat there watching them, not moving, not making a sound.

The night passed with a short rain shower and by morning the sun had reappeared right on schedule.

"Did you hear those wolves last night?" asked Sarge.

"Nope. I slept all night."

"I heard them way down the river, a long way off. Each time I heard them, they were closer. It sounded like they were right here once and then they went the other way up river. I don't know what they were hunting, but it's kind of unusual to have them so close to our camp."

They ate a quick breakfast of pancakes and coffee and got ready for the day ahead. The canoe had a little water in it, so Charlie tipped it on its side and it all ran out. It was once again loaded and they shoved off into the main current.

Just as they started to paddle, the raven flew across the river in front of them and landed on a large rock near the water. Still it made no sound.

The river had calmed down some and the monotonous,

rhythmic paddling had nearly put both of them to sleep. They'd been paddling for nearly 6 hours.

"I could sure use a cup of coffee Charlie. What do ya think?"

"Sounds good to me. My pancakes have worn off too."

They started to look for a spot to stop and in a short while found a place with a nice grassy slope uphill. Sarge was digging in the rucksack and pulled out a can of stew.

"How's this look?"

"Damned good." said Charlie.

Charlie already had a fire going and coffee put together. Sarge just opened the can and set it on a rock near the fire. It didn't take long until they had a meal. As they sat eating, once again they saw the raven, slowly gliding toward them. He landed on a branch near the water and just sat watching, not making a sound.

"I'm about to throw a rock at that thing."

"He's just looking for a handout." said Sarge.

"Don't matter. The damned thing is gettin' on my nerves."

They continued paddling throughout the afternoon, making good time and as the sun started to get nearer the trees, they looked for a place to make camp once again.

"Over there Sarge. It looks like a pretty good place with a flat spot for the tent if we need it."

"Looks pretty good to me too."

They headed the canoe to the river bank and as they got close enough, Charlie stepped out and steadied the canoe for

Sarge. They both stretched. Paddling a canoe for hours at a time sometimes cramped a man's muscles. By now though, they had both toughened up quite a bit.

"Think we need the tent tonight?" asked Charlie.

"I don't think so, but how the hell do ya know?"

They both laughed.

"What's on the menu tonight?" asked Sarge.

"I'm starting to get a bit tired of eating out of a can. How 'bout we use some of the freeze dried stuff. We have 2 packages of Turkey Tetrazzini and about all we need to make a meal is some boiling water to pour on it."

"That sounds pretty good to me."

After a short while the whole area was starting to smell a lot like a fancy restaurant. Both men watched as the dried food turned into a meal fit for a king.

The campsite was cleaned up and the sleeping bags rolled out for the night. As they sat watching the final light of the day fade to darkness, the raven once again came flying silently across the river and landed on the ground near the fire. This had Sarge a bit concerned now since no wild animal ever came near a fire.

"I'm gonna kill that black son of a bitch right now. He's starting to get on my nerves." said Charlie.

He grabbed four good sized rocks and brought back his arm, ready to throw. As the rock flew toward it, the bird stared at Charlie and didn't even move. The first rock sailed past the raven and into the water. Then he took close aim with another and threw hard. The rock sailed close to the big bird's head and again hit the water. The raven remained quiet and didn't move. Then another try with the same result, and then another. Still the large bird sat staring at them, but mostly his eyes were trained on Charlie, one of the men who tried to harm him.

"Damn. You see that Sarge? That damned bird didn't even flinch."

"Ya. I saw that. He just keeps looking at me."

As Charlie turned back to the bird, it was gone. It had only been about 20 feet from them and he missed four times.

"This damned bird is starting to get on my nerves. Ya hear me Sarge?"

The evening passed and morning coffee awoke Charlie early. He poked his head out from his sleeping bag. He was a bit slow at getting moving this morning and Sarge asked him if he wanted his breakfast served in bed. They laughed a bit. Charlie sat up and looked around to see if the raven was still there.

As they drank their last coffee, the raven appeared once more. It drifted slowly toward them over the river, catching the warm air currents, and settled on a branch just a few feet away. His movements weren't like that of a bird. Even the way he turned his head was different. Birds have quick jerky motions, but this one turned his head slowly. Its eyes too were different, with a steady, unblinking gaze.

"This must be the part called 'Bad River'. Dad mentioned it in his journal, but never did say much else except that it was an

Indian burial place and that it went on for a long distance."

"This damned bird really gives me the willies Sarge."

"Ya. I know what ya mean Charlie. Let's paddle hard today and try to get out of this area altogether."

"Sounds like a good plan."

The canoe was loaded under the ever watchful eye of the raven and the two men bent to their task.

The sky was warming and the clouds of late summer provided short periods of shade to cool them off. Near noon they slowed some and just drifted.

"Should we stop for lunch or just keep paddling?" asked Sarge.

"We have a couple biscuits left. Let's just keep paddling and eat on the run. OK?"

"That's fine with me Charlie."

They ate their lunch, drifting sideways in the current. Then it was back to paddling again.

"I gotta take a break Sarge."

They paddled to the nearest shore and Charlie stepped out and walked up the bank to find a spot to take care of business. Sarge too stood nearby watering the flowers. In just a couple minutes he heard a loud yell and Charlie came running down the bank toward the canoe. The look on his face spoke volumes. He was absolutely terrified.

"What the hell is the matter?"

"That damned bird flew down and sat right near me. He was only a couple feet above my head and wasn't a bit scared of me. Let's get out of this place."

Once again they got back in and started paddling, Charlie pulling most of the load. He still, after two hours, had a scared look on his face.

They made several miles in the remainder of the day and Sarge figured that they just had to be out of the Bad River area by now. They were both pretty tired and hungry by late afternoon. Near 6 that evening, they had supper cooking and a large expanse of river to look out over as they ate. There was no raven staring at them and that gave both men a good feeling.

They decided not to put up the tent since the sky was clear with a north wind. That too would keep the mosquitoes away from them as they slept.

Out of the corner of his eye, Sarge caught a movement and turned quickly to face whatever it was. Standing near them was a beautiful young Indian woman. She was dressed in an all white buckskin dress with beautiful quill and bead work up and down the front and the arms.

"Where did you come from?" asked Charlie.

She turned her head slowly and looked over at the river.

"We're on a canoe trip." said Sarge. "Come sit by the fire."

Her eyes were black as coal and she moved slowly. The woman walked over to Sarge and sat close to him, putting her hand on his arm. The men tried to talk to her, but she just smiled and said nothing. She wouldn't even look at Charlie. She smiled when spoken to, but said no words. Most of the time she spent looking into Sarge's face.

After nearly three hours at the fire, Sarge got up to unroll his sleeping bag and the Indian woman came with him to help. He just couldn't figure this thing out. Was this woman some kind of a gift from the river or was she a bad spirit, sent to kill them for being there. Just as quickly as they had rolled out the sleeping bag, the woman laid down and motioned for Sarge to join her. He thought it was a pretty good idea and joined her. There a short distance from the fire, deep in the shadows, they spent the night.

A short time before sunrise, Charlie awoke and looked around. Sarge was still sleeping, but he was alone. He wondered about the woman and where she could have gone.

"You gonna sleep all day?" yelled Charlie.

"Not a bad idea. Where'd she go?"

"No idea Sarge."

"Sure was nice to snuggle up to." he grinned.

The two ate a quick breakfast and loaded the canoe once more. Before Sarge got in, he stopped for a moment and looked around. Seeing no one, he stepped in and they started paddling, neither man having much to say.

The current on the river was fast this day and as they came around a bend in the river they saw her again. She was standing on top of a huge boulder, with a large black raven sitting on her shoulder. She wasn't far from them, so both men could see her very clearly. She still wore the same white buckskin dress with the bead work. Now though she looked very different, She was an old woman, maybe over 80 years old.

Ron Shepherd

She looked at Sarge for a time, eye to eye. Then the raven leaped from her shoulder and flew across the river. When Sarge looked back, the woman was gone.

## Chapter: 11    The Gold Mine

Again the paddling was starting to resemble work to both of them. The supplies were dwindling down to darned few selections from the menu each night. Do you like your beans with or without rice? And your shortcake Sir. Would you like it without strawberries or without raspberries? They kidded each other a lot, but it was starting to get serious. As close as Sarge could figure, he was about a mile from a small town one night and they figured to waste a day getting some supplies. When morning came, they had hidden their canoe and took their empty backpacks for a quick refill. Charlie set a course through the woods and in a matter of just an hour, they were walking into the small town of Edison. There was absolutely nobody around. It appeared as if the whole town had went on holiday.

"What the hell do you expect?" asked Sarge. "It's only 5:00 a.m."

They both started to laugh. Charlie saw a small park bench near the grocery store and motioned for Sarge to come and join him. This little place looked as if it had been designed by Norman Rockwell himself. There were flowers everywhere and brightly colored curtains hanging in the windows. It had the feeling that if you would just walk a short distance and around the corner, you'd never want to come back.

The little town was gradually coming to life. The first thing he saw was a man heading for the outhouse and then a short way over, a woman was taking her dog for a walk. It was nice to see people other than themselves for a change.

There was a small restaurant across the dirt road and Sarge saw someone switch the sign from closed to open. For over two weeks they had been eating from a steel plate or a tin can, but now they wanted a real breakfast.

A cow bell attached to the door rang loudly as they walked into the restaurant..

"Howdy!" said an old man. "You folks want some coffee?"

"Sure." said Charlie. "And a big glass of milk too."

"Same here." said Sarge.

The old man brought them their order and a pair of paper menus. Both sides were hand written and filled with grease spots. There was however some sign of great food. Blueberry pancakes were $2.00 with sausage and coffee. They both ordered the pancakes.

As they sat waiting for their food, Sarge noticed a picture on the wall of a couple G.I.'s. They were Canadian troops that had spent time in Viet Nam. Sarge recalled hearing about their unit. He looked toward the owner.

"You in that picture?"

"Ya. That's me on the left. You ever been there?"

Sarge thought for a bit and didn't want to start any long

conversations.

"No. Not me."

"Damned hot place." said the cook.

In just a few minutes, the man came walking out of the kitchen, loaded with plates.

"Here ya go gentlemen."

He sat the food down in front of them and they attacked like rabid dogs.

"You ever had pancakes that tasted this good?" asked Sarge.

Between bites Charlie mumbled something like "These are great. Should we get shmore?" Sarge laughed and drank his milk, watching his close friend enjoy a good meal. They finished up after a second load and waddled and sloshed across the street to the grocer, a small dog barking at their heels.

When they came back outside, they stood for a while looking up and down the street. This seemed to be the kind of place you just read about in old books. Behind each house there were small gardens, some entirely devoted to flowers. The smells too were most unusual, kind of like lilacs in spring.

After loading what they bought into their backpacks, they headed back to their river camp. The heavy load of food slowed them down some, but in time they found the canoe and got moving once again. Their attitudes had improved dramatically.

The next few days, they made a lot of progress. One after another, they kept finding the landmarks they wanted. Sometimes they were so far apart that they were sure they'd missed them.

"It just can't be that much further now. We only have about five more landmarks and at the rate we been clicking them off, we should be there this week."

Charlie got a big grin on his face. He was really missing his wife and kids.

By the maps that Sarge had brought with him, they were now into the northernmost part of the Northwest Territories. There were no more towns and not even the occasional sound of a train in the distance. The map showed a town named Houton but it was at least 25 miles as the crow flies, and by water it would be twice that. Sarge and Charlie, by training, always had an escape route planned and lurking in the back of their minds. If things got tough, you had to have a backup plan.

It had been quite a few weeks since they had seen the inside of a barber shop and they were starting to resemble some pretty tough looking characters. Sarge had a tan that made him look a lot like Charlie and got kidded sometimes about being his long lost brother. Charlie was normally a pretty big character, but with all this paddling, he had lost what little fat he had brought with him. Drugs had now taken a back seat for both men, but still neither of them talked about it. The subject of drugs seemed to be still a bit too tender.

As they sat by the fire one evening, Charlie finally broke the ice.

"Ya know Sarge, this is the first time in years that drugs haven't been in my thoughts night and day. I'm not saying that

I have it licked, but I am starting to heal up some."

Sarge just sat there for a while.

"I used to get a bit stressed and the first thing that I thought of was a load of heroin. Now I'm a long ways past that. I don't even get stressed any more. I have to admit though, that damned bird really gave me the shakes."

They both laughed at themselves.

"I was checking out the maps a while ago. We only have two landmarks left and who knows where we'll find them. We have gone through a pile of different rivers and never missed a mark. For all we know, tomorrow might be the end of the trip.!" said Sarge.

Charlie perked up some and moved closer to the fire.

"Ya know Sarge. I been thinking about my wife and kids. I ain't been much of a provider for them, but this trip might just change all that. We could move into a nice house and into a good neighborhood. That would mean that the kids would get a good education too. My wife has worked so darned hard just to keep us fed and I spent a lot of that on drugs."

He hung his head a bit but then in just a few seconds, he was right back with his chin up talking about the future.

Another thing that was starting to bother him was that if he didn't make it home from this trip, who would take care of them!

"We need to be a bit more positive Charlie. We're both going to make it home, and that's the end of this conversation."

Charlie got to his feet. He looked like a giant from where

Sarge sat. His huge form was back-lighted by a cloud of sparks coming up from the fire. His voice was strong and steady and nearly boomed at Sarge.

"Like hell this is the end of this conversation."

Sarge had been laying next to the fire resting his head on his hand. The sudden and explosive words from Charlie got his attention.

"We need to get this thing straightened out between us and now is the right time." said Charlie.

"What is it that you want to do?"

"I want you and I to make an agreement. If I don't make it home from this trip, I want my share to go to my wife and I'll do the same thing for you."

"Why you big oaf. Sure I'll do that, but we don't need any kind of an agreement. I'd do my best for you Charlie, no matter what happens."

Charlie started to calm down some. He had wanted to help his family and this seemed to be the only chance he'd have.

They paddled hard for six more days and were starting to think that they'd missed a landmark. They had seen sights that most men would never see, or much less believe.

On one especially warm morning, they came around a turn in the river to see a half dozen wolves trying desperately to bring down a cow moose. She kicked hard and sent one sailing out into the river. We paddled silently past the carnage. It was a pretty sure thing that she'd lose the fight, and the wolves no doubt ate her from nose to tail.

# To Waltz With A White Horse

As they sat one evening studying the maps, it was becoming apparent that they had passed out of Canada and were now just barely into Alaska. They still were going in a northwesterly direction and the river was getting wider, faster and deeper.

Next morning, they had only been paddling for a couple hours when they found the next landmark. There was only one to go. Their supplies were still in good shape but they needed to eat more fish if they were to make it last.

They turned to the west and followed a small stream for a couple hours. The next landmark was a five foot wide round rock sitting on a small granite ledge on the left side of the river as they paddled.

"Sarge? Sarge? Sarge, there it is. There's the damned rock."

"You're right Charlie. Damn. You are right."

They pulled the canoe up close to the bank and Charlie just stepped out into the cold water. They had made it at last. This was where the gold mine was supposed to be.

They emptied the canoe and placed all of their gear up on the bank a short distance. The surrounding area was mountainous and the sky was as blue as Maggie's eyes. The beach as far as they could see, was small pebbles, almost black in color.

"Smell that air Sarge. It's clean and pure, no pollution."

Behind them was a small wooded knoll with a few large trees to block the wind. They spent nearly the whole day setting camp. This was going to be their home for a while and they might just as well be comfortable.

That night, they built themselves a good meal of fresh salmon from the river and a can of creamed corn. Charlie had a good recipe for biscuits and he cooked them a large batch.

"Any idea of where we go from here?" asked Charlie.

"Well, as far as I can tell, it should be right in this very area. We'll have to look around tomorrow."

"You mean it ain't just stacked up ready for us to load?"

"Don't suppose we'll be that lucky." and they laughed.

They sat for a bit longer than usual enjoying the flames and the fact that they had made it to the mine. They talked of what they would do with the gold and it seemed that Sarge didn't have much to say about that.

"You act like this stuff is no big thing Sarge. What's going on inside that head of yours?"

"Well, Charlie, I'd like to be rich just like the next guy, but I already got everything that a man needs. Some old goat used to say that money can't buy happiness, but I doubt that he ever had a gold mine."

They both laughed.

"I guess I already have the best things myself."

They stood up and started to clean up the campsite. There was still a few biscuits and Charlie threw them off into the darkness of the woods.

"That wasn't such a good idea!" said Sarge. "We sure don't need any bears around our camp. They get pretty damned big around this part of the world."

"Can't believe that I did that. All I was thinking about was giving the birds something to pick at. I'll clean that up in the morning as soon as I get up." said Charlie.

They slept in the tent because it was starting to look like it might rain. Usually they just rolled up in their blankets and called wherever they were, home. It didn't take too long until they were both asleep.

Morning found Sarge up early staring into the flames of the fire. A pot of coffee was making the whole world smell good. He'd gotten water from the stream and found it to be as clear and good tasting as any he'd ever drank. While he waited for the coffee, he looked around at the countryside. The tips of the mountains were just starting to show a hint of sunshine and by the looks of things, they already had a lot of snow. The birds were making quite a racket, like they were trying to out-sing each other. A pair of eagles swooped down low to the water and one caught a small fish. The whole place was beautiful.

Charlie usually was up and looking for the coffee as soon as it got light, but today, he just decided to sleep a few more minutes.

"You waiting for me to bring you breakfast in bed you old goat?" yelled Sarge.

Charlie opened the tent zipper and stuck out his face.

"I'll take steak and eggs, and a couple pancakes." said Charlie. "I haven't slept this good in a long time."

He stumbled up to the fire and sat down on a small log.

"This is sure the prettiest place I've ever seen." He gazed off at the mountains. "Look at the way the blues and grays fade into the snow line."

"Just a few minutes ago, a cow moose and her calf walked across the river. They sure didn't seem to be too scared of us."

"They're pretty darned big though."

"Today, we better get a few things done. The first thing is to get out the maps and try to see where we are." said Sarge. "If we get a lot of gold, we'll have to figure a way to get it out."

"I guess I just thought we'd paddle back home."

"First thing is that we'd be paddling against the current the entire trip. That would seem like paddling five times as far. We wouldn't make it home before winter. In addition to that, we'd probably spend quite a while paddling upstream through the Bad River area."

Charlie stood up. He had a funny look in his face. It seemed as if he might have already had enough of that place.

"I better go find them biscuits before the bears do."

He walked to where he thought the biscuits were and in just a short time he yelled.

"Get over her Sarge."

"What the hell you want?"

"Look at this."

Sarge walked over to Charlie and saw him bent down, looking at something on the ground.

"Looks like we had visitors."

"Looks to me like we had three visitors." said Sarge.

There in the soft earth were the tracks of one large bear and a pair of cubs. The big tracks measured nearly a foot from claw to heel. The bears came within just a couple yards of their tent while they were asleep. Now, the problem was that of them returning for more of Charlie's biscuits. It had the makings of a bad situation. Just having a bear hang around for food was one thing, but a couple cubs spelled a disaster in the making.

"What the hell do we do now?" asked Charlie.

"Well, this is where the gold is. We can't just get into the canoe and paddle away. I still have the pistol if we need it. A .357 Magnum isn't much of a bear gun, but it might scare them off and give us enough time to get away. Did you bring a gun Charlie?"

"No, and as big as that bear is, an RPG wouldn't be enough." he chuckled softly.

"We do have a problem now Charlie. That bear is a sow with cubs. You don't want to ever be around a situation like that. If she comes back for more biscuits, there'll be hell to pay."

"Ya. I hear ya talkin' Sarge." He had a most serious tone to his voice.

They had only been there for a short while and had already gotten themselves in trouble. They'd have to be a lot more careful in the future.

"Which way do you think we should go? This looks like an awful big place." said Charlie.

"Well, the first thing we have to remember is that when he worked the gold, he probably needed to have water. That means we stay close to this river when we look."

The two headed downstream looking for any sign that Sarge's dad had been there. They spent the entire day and never found so much as a nail. It was as if nobody had ever been there before. By evening they were both pretty tired and supper was a can of beans and that was good enough for each of them. As they sat by the fire, it seemed that they were both a bit depressed. It was like they had both figured that it was just a matter of loading it into the canoe.

"Damn. If I'd been the one who found the gold, I'd have done nearly anything to hide the fact that I'd ever been there." said Sarge.

Charlie sat bolt upright, a new sparkle in his eyes.

"Ya know Sarge, I think you may have something there. This is the place he brought us to and this is where the gold is. Now we just gotta find it."

"I think we should start by panning tomorrow. We'll take a scoop of dirt and wash it down. It may take a while, but I know we can do it."

The plan was set. Tomorrow they'd be a lot closer to finding the gold.

Around midnight, they both awoke with a start when they heard a low "whuff" sound near them. They knew it was the bear for sure, back for more biscuits. Sarge grabbed his .357 and held it tightly in his hand, ready for whatever came his way. Charlie stayed where he was, not making a sound. After a short while, something moved the wall of the tent and Sarge brought up the revolver, ready to squeeze off a string of six if he needed to. The intruder moved off into the brush and within a short while it was all quiet again.

The morning found Sarge and Charlie checking for tracks. They were the same as before. One large sow and a pair of big cubs. Those bears were fed here once and they wanted more of Charlie's home cooking.

The campfire felt especially good on this morning. The temperature had fallen to less than freezing and it was just a hint of things to come. When winter closed in, that was the end of any thoughts of gold. In this part of the world winter started with huge amounts of snow and by the time you couldn't move any more, the cold set in. Temperatures could fall a hundred degrees in one day. Sixty-five below zero was certainly not unheard of. At that temperature if you could spit on the ground, it would make a popping sound, freezing solid before it landed.

The only mode of travel would be a sled and dog team and even then, you better know what you're doing. Men that carried the mail sometimes were found in the spring frozen to death inside their tents with their dog teams eaten by packs of wolves.

They talked for quite a while about winter survival and deep inside each man wondered if they had what it would take to make it.

Charlie headed upstream with a shovel and a gold pan and Sarge went the other way. They planned on being back in camp near noon for a meal.

Around midday Sarge came back into the camp and built up

the fire to boil some coffee. Near 1:30 Charlie still wasn't there. At 2:00 Sarge went looking for him. He walked almost a mile, yelling for Charlie nearly the whole way, and then he heard a muffled reply. It was Charlie and he was close by.

Sarge started to walk toward the voice and he looked up to see a huge bear and two cubs digging at a small hole in a cliff face. He could hear Charlie yelling for him and it seemed that it was right near the nose of the bear. Sarge looked around and saw a small tree with a lot of branches and even with his fake leg, managed to get up a short ways. As soon as he was far enough up to where he thought that the bear couldn't get him, he settled on a limb and took out the revolver. He aimed just over the bears head and squeezed the trigger.

The resultant noise the bear made, nearly rolled him right out of the tree. Then he fired again, but a bit closer. This time the big bear gave out a loud woof and all three ran back toward the river. It had seemed that she didn't know where the noise came from. Calm returned back to their little spot of ground and in just a few minutes, Charlie came crawling out of the hole, still shaking badly.

"What the hell were you doing in that hole?" asked Sarge.

"Well, I was digging around looking for gold and when I looked up, one of those damned cubs was right next to me. I looked around and saw the big sow just ten yards or so away. I knew I was dead meat."

Sarge was still up in the tree trying to get down without killing himself.

"Then what happened?"

"About the only thing I could do was to take off on a dead run back to the camp, but that big bear was right behind me all the way. She tripped me once and tried to bite off my head. I pretended to be dead and when she walked off a ways, I got up again and ran like hell. Then I looked up and saw this hole in the ground and just dove right in. She was so close I could smell her." Charlie had a different expression on his face.

Sarge came slowly back down the tree, one limb at a time until he got back to earth safe and sound.

"Well, that explains what you were doing in the hole I guess, but if I'd have waited much longer, she would have dug you out." Sarge laughed.

"Didn't matter." He turned his face away from Sarge.

"What the hell do you mean it didn't matter?"

"Didn't matter to me, cuz I'da died a rich man." His voice was almost like a hushed growl.

Sarge's eyes brightened up.

"Look at this." and Charlie reached in his pocket.

In his outstretched hand he held a gold nugget that must have weighed a half a pound. Charlie had found the mine.

"Lemme see that." said Sarge and he reached for the gold.

Charlie pulled his hand back like he didn't want Sarge to see it. He had a strange look in his eye like he was going a bit crazy. Sarge figured that it was just from the close call with the bear. His feelings toward Charlie changed though in that moment, as he saw the inside of his mind. It was laid open for the whole world to see. At that very moment, Charlie seemed like he could have killed Sarge just for that small nugget in his hand and it scared him some.

Sarge got down and crawled inside. There were shovels and all kinds of equipment. There was a sluice box and a small pile of pure gold nuggets. His dad had hidden everything well, covering the entrance with small trees. They had indeed found the gold.

Darkness descended upon their camp and there was little conversation. Sarge was still trying to figure out what had happened with Charlie. It might have been the close call with the bear, but he wasn't sure. Sometimes gold brings out the worst in a man.

When morning came, it wasn't the usual conversation they'd been used to for so many weeks. It seemed that they were almost strangers. They ate some breakfast and headed off to see if they could get more gold out of the mine. There was only so much that they could put into the canoe anyway. Sarge noticed a welt behind Charlie's ear and asked him what happened. He didn't seem too sure how it happened except that the bear tripped him and bit him in the head. Then he got up and ran some more. Charlie just didn't want to talk about it though and started to walk to the mine.

They widened out the opening some so they could get inside easier. The mine ran in a straight line in about 25 feet and stopped. Sarge lit a candle and the whole place seemed to be covered with gold nuggets. They were easily picked out of the dirt and in just a short time they had more than they could carry back to the camp. It was a quiet trip with no conversation. They gathered up some more firewood and put on a pot of coffee.

"Now what do we do?" asked Sarge. "By tomorrow, we'll have all we can carry back home."

Charlie didn't answer him. He just sat staring into the fire. He turned to face Sarge and it was as if this good friend had turned into a stranger. Sarge tried joking with him a little, but it got no response. This had him a bit worried.

By the end of the next day, they had all the gold that they could transport out by canoe. Sarge figured that they should head back the next day. Cold was starting to make its way into their camp and snow might not be far off. There was no longer any casual conversation. Sarge told Charlie what to do and sometimes he followed orders and sometimes he didn't, but in any case there was still no conversation.

Morning found them loading up. The canoe was in the water tied to a rock. Sarge bent over to move his backpack and he saw a movement next to him. He ducked and Charlie hit him a glancing blow with a large piece of driftwood. Then he swung again and missed. Sarge elbowed Charlie in the ribs and that stiffened him up enough for him to get away. The whole thing came as a great surprise to him. It just didn't seem like the kind of thing Charlie would do.

Charlie straightened up and ran away toward the mine. The thing that surprised Sarge most was the look on his face. He had no expression at all. There should have at least been some anger.

Sarge dragged the canoe up on the bank, still trying to figure out what had just happened. It was a sure thing though that Charlie had just tried to kill him. Why, was the real question now. Just a couple days ago they had made a promise to each other that if either one didn't make it home, their family would be taken care of. What happened? What had changed?

That night Sarge sat by the fire waiting for Charlie to come back. He thought back to when he was in Viet Nam. His squad had set up an ambush for the Viet Cong and were waiting quietly. After a couple hours, the men were getting anxious for something to happen and Sarge had a hard time keeping the lid on them. Then in an instant, the air filled with the sound of small arms fire. Someone had heard a mouse or something and fired a shot. All hell broke loose then with each man laying down a string of defensive fire. They were shooting at ghosts and nothing more.

Around midnight as he sat listening to the river and the wind in the pines, he heard the sound of someone close by. It was someone taking soft small steps. He started to turn and then everything went black for a moment. Charlie had hit him in the head with something and he was bleeding. He lay there half conscious looking past the fire at Charlie getting the canoe ready. Just as Charlie was about to shove it into the water, Sarge yelled.

"What the hell are you doing?"

He drew his revolver and aimed it at Charlie.

"Now this is as far as it's going to go. Pull the canoe back up on the beach."

Sarge could feel the blood running down his back from a bad cut on his head. This time Charlie did as he was told, but still there was no talking, no expression.

"Now come here by the fire and sit down."

Charlie looked over at Sarge and then took off running again back toward the mine. In the dark, Sarge could hear him falling every few steps, but that didn't stop him. He ran like a madman.

After a short while, Sarge built up the fire and went to the river to clean up his head wound. He washed it with soap and water and then wrapped some gauze around his head. Every time he bent down it felt as if he would blank out.

It was near 1:00 a.m. when he heard Charlie coming again. This time he made no attempt to be quiet. He came running with the force of a freight train, a large chunk of wood raised over his head. Charlie had a fierce look on his face, but Sarge was ready this time.

"Charlie." he yelled loudly. "Don't do it."

He was within only ten feet when Sarge pulled the trigger. The gun belched smoke and a large ball of flame and Charlie fell dead right next to Sarge. He never made another move and calm returned once more to the river.

## Chapter: 12    Murder

Daylight found Sarge sitting by the fire trying to figure out what to do next. He had the maps unfolded in the sand. It seemed that if he continued downstream for another few days, he'd find a place where a road crossed the river. A town would still be a long way off though. He might be able to flag down a car for a ride. As close as he could figure there were at least three days of hard paddling.

He had rolled Charlie up in a small canvas and tied it shut with some rope. He'd seen men lose it before, but this was totally unexpected. Charlie had been a close and a trusted friend. He was positive that it wasn't the gold though. Charlie had a bad welt behind his ear and that may have caused an aneurism. Only an autopsy could tell. The only thing for him to do now was to load the canoe with Charlie, the gold and a few supplies. It would be a hard trip and he planned on paddling as long as he could see.

## To Waltz With A White Horse

He got Charlie into the canoe and placed what gold he could carry into the bottom of the canoe in small sacks. He left the tent hidden in the mine and did his best to remove all traces that they'd ever been there. He shoved off at 7:00 in the morning and the current took him miles from the mine in just a short time. It sure felt bad thinking that Charlie's family wouldn't have him in their lives any more. He'd wasted a good man and way back in the deepest recesses of his mind, he wondered if he had really needed to kill Charlie. Was he really trying to kill him? There were so very many unanswered questions.

Sarge paddled hard all day and when it got so dark he couldn't see any more, he went ashore and built a small fire to cook something for supper. The clouds covered the sky making it so dark that he knew he'd have to wait until morning. It was a long night for him.

Sarge took out his journal and started to write about what had happened. He said that it was kill or be killed and his love of life must have been greater than Charlie's. He also spoke of how it might change the way Maggie looked at him. She wouldn't want to spend her life with a killer.

Inside he thought for a time about what his father might have done in the same situation. He felt a small degree of justification knowing that he would have handled the situation exactly the same way.

He thought too of those beautiful kids of his. They sure did love their Dad, drugs and all. How could this have happened?

The next morning, he was still tired from spending too much time thinking the night before. He made coffee and drank the whole pot.

The current in the river moved by at a terribly fast rate. He was quite fatigued inside and out, and the thoughts of having killed his friend still wore hard on him. Each time he closed his eyes, he could see Charlie coming at him with murder in his eyes.

He pushed the canoe into the water and started paddling again. The current wore him out in a short time. He would have thought that going downstream would have been easier, but it just wasn't the case.

Later in the day he thought he could hear a rapids ahead and tried hard to slow the canoe. It was just too difficult for him and he was swept along like a leaf in a gale. Ahead he could see the rapids, but there was nothing he could do. His thoughts raced downstream ahead of him. He couldn't even steer to the river bank. Sarge wasn't much of a praying man, but here, on this particular day, he asked the Creator to spare him.

Ahead were boulders the size of houses with the river winding in and out of them making his efforts seem weak against such a force. All he could do was use his paddle to push away from them. Even that seemed futile. Then in just a few short minutes, it was over. He had survived the rapids and thanked the Creator for sparing him.

At his first chance, he beached the canoe and pulled it up on shore a short distance. This was the hardest day he'd had, and from what he could figure, it would only get worse. He sat on the river bank for a while, thinking about the river. After a cold biscuit and some water he shoved off once again. The rest of the day, he went in and out of small rapids, but it was nothing he couldn't handle.

Nighttime again was too dark to paddle so he built a fire and tried to get some sleep. He reached into his pack and pulled out his .357 magnum, the gun he'd killed Charlie with. It felt cold to the touch.

Sleep came at last. During the night, the level of the river rose another couple feet. There had to be a storm somewhere upstream to cause such a great change.

When he awoke, it was daylight and starting to rain lightly. He hadn't slept well in a long time, so when he finally did get to sleep, he caught up on what he'd missed. There wasn't much left for groceries so he opened a can of beans and sat it on a rock near the fire to heat. In a short time, they were warm enough and he ate quickly, not even tasting it, not wanting to waste daylight.

Sarge put the .357 on his belt, in case he might need it. There was no telling when he might just meet another bear face to face.

Again he pushed off and continued downstream. Now the water seemed to be moving faster than ever and his efforts at paddling in a straight line were getting him nowhere. He wasn't sure where he was going, but he was sure going there fast. It just seemed like someone else was in control. He looked down at the body and noticed that there was a large black stain where Charlie's blood had leaked through. It sickened him some. It was one thing to cap some gook in the jungle, but to kill a friend seemed so very terrible and a complete failure on his own part.

At around noon, the sky cleared. He had been making good time, no thanks to his paddling efforts. Around him on the river bank, it was starting to look more like big boulders scattered around and not the sandy beach look of before. There were small birds that seemed to be following him. Maybe they were waiting for a meal of Charlie. Funny how animals can smell death he thought.

As he paddled, his thoughts turned for a time back to Maggie. She was the only good thing that had happened to him in years. She seemed to be so very far away right now. He could see her face and almost feel the softness of her hand. A splash of cold river water brought him back to the seriousness of his situation and he paddled with even more determination.

The river started to pick up speed again and the rocks started to grow in size and frequency. It was as if he was being poured out of a bottle and there wasn't a thing he could do but pray and paddle. So again, right before he was pushed into the mouth of the beast, he asked for help.

The current continued to move faster and then he saw what looked like the end of the river. There were no more boulders and the whole thing looked smooth even though he was moving fast. Then he saw the unspeakable. He was just seconds from going over a waterfall. As he got to the edge, the first thing he saw was the bottom, over twenty feet down. The rest was blurred badly. He and the canoe parted company around half way to the bottom. He wasn't sure about the rest.

When he awoke, he was laying in shallow water with the falls nowhere in sight. He was coughing badly and tried to pull himself up on shore. The water was colder than anything he had ever known. His head had a large cut that was bleeding down his left cheek. He was a bit dizzy and when he tried to stand, it became evident that his artificial leg and he had parted company as well. He was, as he used to say, "in shit shape" and he'd have bet anything that it was going to get worse before things improved. He still had the .357 strapped to his side with his knife, and his billfold was still in his back pocket. There was a small container of stick matches and a couple quarters. He still had his jacket too, one item that just might save his life. That was the sum total of his worldly possessions. As he sat there assessing his situation, he remembered his 12 weeks in survival school. Those were some of the hardest days he'd ever spent, but he found out what he was made of and he was satisfied with what he saw. He could do this.

The first thing was to find something to use as a crutch. Then he had to build a fire and dry out or face hypothermia, not a pleasant thought. He built up the fire and then took all of the wet clothes off. He hung them close to the fire and then as they were drying, he stood near the flames, turning around and around like a chicken on a barbecue. The heat was starting to warm him, even on the inside where he really needed it. The next time he went to turn his clothes, the shirt was dry so he put it on. Gradually he was getting dressed again. It was nearing dark before he got it done. He slept little that night and kept the fire going brightly.

By morning, he had a plan. He'd look for anything that had survived the falls. He found nothing, not even Charlie. The maps, the gold, his journal, the food, all were gone, swept downstream to who knows where. The indestructible canoe was of little value since he couldn't even find parts of it.

The branch he was using for a crutch seemed adequate, but he had to carve a better fit for his armpit and that took him quite a while. This done he started to climb out and away from the rocky shore of the river.

His trip up to the ridge took him most of the day and by sunset, he was hungry and needed rest. Hypothermia was still his worst enemy and it had to be dealt with. The first thing was that he needed a fire. That done, he started to make a shelter of balsam boughs. Then it was a matter of gathering grass and reeds to make a bed and blanket. Everything took twice as long as it should, since he now only had one leg. Even getting up off the ground seemed to be a monumental task. Near 9:00 he really needed some sleep. He felt exhausted and the hunger pains were doing their best to keep his attention. He thought of the bugs he'd been taught about. They were a totally disgusting thought, but if worse came to worse, he could and would eat them.

# To Waltz With A White Horse

The next day was spent stumbling down the river bank looking for anything that had survived the falls. He found a piece of string and what looked like a piece of the canoe, a small piece. As he searched, he kept thinking he'd find Charlie's body, but it wasn't to be. He had no idea what he'd do with it anyway.

He saw a school of fish in shallow water and drew his revolver to try to kill one. He only had the six shots it held and he'd better not waste any of them. He aimed carefully at the one closest to the surface and slowly squeezed the trigger. The majority of the fish just swam away, but one turned belly up and came to the surface. As he started to go toward it, he noticed that it was drifting away downstream, faster than he could manage to walk. His meal was being swept away by the current and was out of sight in just a few minutes. Again he built a fire and made some shelter. He sat thinking about Maggie. Would she still love him after learning that he had killed Charlie? He warmed himself sufficiently and slept off and on through the night.

As the morning sky started to lighten some, it began to rain lightly and within just an hour it had turned to slushy snow. Things were looking pretty bad, but he'd survived worse. The first thing to remember was that he had to have a plan, a direction, a goal. He huddled in his small shelter, trying to decide whether or not to head out. The snow and rain had turned the ground into a muddy mess and he didn't want to fall and break a bone. He decided to stay put.

Around 8:00 in the morning he heard a shot, and it didn't seem much more than half a mile away. He marked the position in his head and just as he was standing, he heard another, confirming the direction. The .357 would make a lot of noise, and someone might find him, but what if he wasted the bullets and he was still lost. He put it back into the holster.

He raised to full height and started to walk in a southerly direction, but not making very good time. He knew that he had to hurry. If it were hunters like he thought it was, they might leave the area soon.

He moved as fast as a one legged man could, and within two hours, he came to what appeared to be the fresh gut pile of a caribou. He poked at it with a small stick, looking for the liver. Then he thought he'd better hurry to find who fired the shots. The bloody drag trail led downhill just a short distance and it looked like the animal was loaded into a truck and two men got inside, driving away to who knows where. The only thing he could do was to follow the tire tracks no matter how far they lead him.

Within another hour, he was wishing that he had taken the liver and heart from the gut pile. He was damned hungry, but he knew he could go another couple days without food. After a brief rest, he stood to go and then he heard voices.

"Hey! Hey! I need some help!"

"Over here." someone yelled.

"I need some help."

A couple guys dressed in red came running toward him.

Sarge just sat down on the ground and tried desperately to control his emotions.

"You lost?" said one of them.

"Well, it's a long story. Ya got any food?" he asked.

One guy got on each side and they darned near carried Sarge over to their camp. They set him down in a folding chair and within a minute, handed him some coffee with cream and sugar and a peanut butter sandwich. Food never tasted so good before. After an hour of getting settled in, Sarge told the two hunters most of the truth. He left out the part about killing Charlie and the gold mine they'd found.

"Any chance I could get a ride to the nearest town? I need to talk to a Sheriff."

The men looked at each other wondering what they had stumbled into. They had gotten all the game they had come for so going back wasn't out of the question. It was a long trip of over 30 miles through some pretty bad country, but they had four wheel drive. Sarge could ride in the back seat.

When they arrived at Wolf Creek, they dropped Sarge off at the Sheriff's Office and helped him through the door. The Sheriff came into the room and met him with outstretched hands. He wanted that .357 Magnum, and then they could talk.

"I need a place to sit officer. I got a long story to tell you."

Sarge started by telling about him and Charlie and how they were looking for gold. He said that they found some and Charlie went crazy and tried to kill him, so he shot him, killing him with one shot. Then he told of how he loaded everything including Charlie into the canoe and how he went over the falls losing everything. The whole story took a long time to tell, but the Sheriff seemed to be a good listener.

"Those two hunters picked me up and brought me here."

Sarge wasn't in too good of shape right then. He had three one hundred dollar bills in his wallet and not even a change of clothes. Wolf creek was a town of nearly a thousand people and a few stores. He bought some clothes and found a rooming house to take him in for a couple days. At the clinic, he found a pair of crutches. His last purchase was a razor and a toothbrush. He was set now. The Sheriff had told him not to leave town until they had this all sorted out.

The next day, the Sheriff sent out a couple deputies to the waterfall, the place that Sarge darned near lost his life. They came back with Sarge's leg and one canoe paddle. Nothing else, and no body. Without a body, there was little else to talk about. Sarge was free to leave the next day, but the Sheriff wanted to know his address and phone number just in case he would be needed later.

He made arrangements to fly back to Minnesota. He was part of the cargo on a bush pilots run to International Falls. He had a lot of time to think on the flight back. He was getting concerned about the Sheriff asking his address and phone number. He'd only done what was necessary to save his own life.

As they crossed back into the United States, he let out an audible sigh of relief. He was only a hundred miles or so from home now. He hired a guy at the airport to drive him back home.

When he walked into the bar, he saw Maggie and she almost knocked over three guys getting to him.

"Oh Sarge. I've missed you so much."

She kissed and hugged him and after things calmed down some, he said that he had to go to the house and call Charlie's wife.

"Where is Charlie?" she asked.

"I killed him."

Maggie was the only one close enough to hear that and she followed him to the house. He picked up the phone and dialed.

"Charlie's dead." he said to the phone. "He went crazy after a bear almost got him and he tried to kill me three times. Hello. Hello."

"Maggie. Can you make me a pot of coffee. We gotta talk."

They spent a long time talking. Maggie was a good listener and the pair shared a pile of tears.

"I can't believe that I killed that guy. Charlie was a good friend and we shared some damned tough times." said Sarge.

"Do you think there'll be any trouble with the law?"

"The Sheriff didn't seem too concerned since they didn't find the body."

"I sure hope that doesn't change."

"Well, whatever happens, I sure hope you'll be there with me. I can't imagine ever going through the rest of my life without you." said Sarge.

She hugged him and promised to stick with him.

"When do you have to be back in Illinois?" asked Sarge.

Maggie's eyes opened wide and she started laughing.

"I guess I might have forgotten one little thing. I resigned my commission and now this is where I get my mail."

Sarge seemed to come unglued. What he thought would take two more years, had happened while he was gone. Maggie was his and she wouldn't have to leave ever again.

As the days rolled by, it was starting to look like things would settle down again. The bar was doing well and Sarge was making a bit of money to put in the bank. Maggie and him were starting to talk of things like weddings.

Winter was making its presence known and it seemed to snow almost every day. Maggie put a plow on the front of her pickup and spent a lot of time plowing driveways and parking lots. She was good at it and made a lot of money. She however refused to charge some of her clients because she knew they were having a tough time.

During the last part of January the temperatures never got above zero. They used an awful pile of wood in the bar's fireplace. Sometimes when it got close to noon, the regulars would come in and instead of drinking a beer, they'd pull up a chair near the fireplace and just sit and talk. It seemed that the community gathering place was right in front of their fireplace. Sarge had come up with a winter drink idea that helped a lot in paying for the firewood. He served hot brandy and gave each person their own nutmeg nut. They took out their knives and shaved in as much as they liked. All they had to do when they came in was to take out the nut and set it on the bar. The bartender poured the appropriate ingredients and the holder of the prized nut would scrape and shave some into his mug. It didn't seem to matter if a little pocket lint went into the mix.

Sarge and Maggie had talked of getting married in the spring. There were so many friends and relatives that said they would come to the wedding, that there was no place to house all of them. The day was set for June 3rd. Maggie would be a June bride.

The hard days of winter were gradually taking a back seat to the warmth of spring. The whole place was starting to turn green and the towering snow banks had finally disappeared. On the south side of the bar, a surprise bunch of tulips reached up and bloomed brightly for all to see. Winter's back had been broken.

Plans for the wedding were coming along nicely. Sarge and Maggie had sat down together and written up their vows. Each one had something special they wanted to say. The wedding would take place over by the river. Some teenagers had been hired to mow all the grass and cut some brush down. It looked like a park with the mighty Bigfork in the background.

The wedding was getting closer and the level of excitement was growing each day. Now they were down to things like wedding dresses and food.

One evening as the local patrons were celebrating the first Friday of the week, the local sheriff walked in. A few looked up, but he was getting to be a regular so they didn't pay too much attention to him. Maggie was playing pool and watched as he walked up to Sarge. The whole place went silent and all could hear the conversation.

"William Stone. I am arresting you for the murder Charles Wilson. Here are the extradition papers from Wolf Creek, Alaska."

They were standing close to each other and then the Sheriff reached behind him and took out a pair of handcuffs. Sarge held out his hands and was handcuffed.

He told Maggie that he loved her and was quite unceremoniously lead outside and put into the back of the squad car. There was little or no conversation.

Back in the bar, Maggie was crying and all the jailhouse attorneys were quoting the law to her. Each had their say about how they couldn't do that to him, but he was for damned sure gone anyway, headed for Wolf Creek, Alaska. There were a lot of things that needed to be taken care of and the wedding would have to be postponed for who knows how long.

Maggie closed up early and went right to bed, her mind going in several directions all at the same time. There had to be something that she could do to get him out of this situation. She really didn't know much about the law, but had a feeling that she'd be learning fast.

The next afternoon, Sarge was flown to Wolf Creek and put in their small jail. It looked like one of those places you used to see in the old western movies. There were only four cells and

Sarge was the only occupant.

The Sheriff came in to talk to him.

"I heard that they call you Sarge. Well Sarge, if you don't give me any trouble, I'll leave your cell door open. Don't give me any reason to regret this now. Ya hear?

"I won't Sheriff and thank you."

"You have to be in court tomorrow for arraignment and that's at 10:00. After that, it's a matter of waiting for a trial date. If they find you guilty, you'll be transferred to a bigger facility."

"Can you tell me a little of what brought all this on?" asked Sarge.

"Well, about the only thing I can tell you is that they found Charles Wilson's body this spring a couple miles from the falls you went down. They did an autopsy and found the .357 slug in his body, just like you said."

"He was doing his level best to kill me Sheriff and he tried three times. The third time, I had to shoot him or get killed myself."

"Well Sarge, I guess it will all come out at the trial. If it all happened the way you said, you might stand a chance, but from what I've seen so far, you're dead meat."

With that, the Sheriff went back to his desk and got to work on something else, leaving Sarge thinking and wondering.

In the morning Sarge was taken next door to the courtroom. He had no attorney. There were a couple others there taking notes and then the Judge walked in and a bailiff said "All Rise,"

The entire room came to its feet.

"Please be seated." he said.

The Judge looked over some papers and stared directly at Sarge.

"William Stone, you're charged with first degree murder, more precisely, the murder of Charles Wilson. How do you plead?"

Sarge stood to his full height.

"Not guilty Your Honor."

All was quiet in the courtroom for quite a while as the Judge shuffled through some papers.

"Trial is set for Monday June 25 in this courtroom. Will you be represented by an attorney?"

"I sure hope so Your Honor, but I don't know any attorneys in the area. Can I get one from somewhere else?"

"You sure can young man, but just remember that he has to be licensed to practice here in Alaska." said the Judge.

"Yes Sir. Can I be released on bail?"

"Considering the nature of the crime that you're charged with, bail is granted at $250,000. Any further questions?"

"No Your Honor."

With that, the Judge tapped his gavel and the courtroom cleared.

With bail being set so high, there was absolutely no chance he could get out to await trial.

Sarge was lead back to the jail in handcuffs and as soon as they went inside, the Sheriff took them back off.

"I'm going to need to make a few phone calls Sheriff."

"Any time you need to call, just use that phone in the corner. You have to reverse the charges or it won't work."

"Thanks Sheriff. I appreciate it."

Around 6:00 they brought him a tray of food covered by another tray. It came complete with bread and butter and a cup of coffee. The food wasn't actually too bad. Much better he was sure, than scavenging through a caribou gut pile.

After he ate, he called Maggie.

"Maggie?"

"Sarge?"

"Ya it's me alright. I'm in jail in Wolf Creek. I need an attorney that's licensed to practice here in Alaska."

"Now that's a mighty big order but I might just be able to help you. You never asked what my Dad did for a living did you?

"No I guess I didn't"

"Well, he's an attorney and a damned good one."

"That probably won't help me much, he has to be licensed to practice here in Alaska. I'm going to have one hell of a time finding one."

Maggie gave a little laugh.

"Dad was a federal attorney Sarge. That means that he can practice in every state and possession of the United States. I'll go and talk to him tomorrow and then I want you to call me back the same time tomorrow. OK?"

"Sounds good to me Maggie. Remember I love you."

"I love you too Sarge."

And with that, Sarge finally found a bit of hope in an otherwise hopeless situation.

## Chapter: 13    Wolf Creek, Alaska

Maggie was up early the next day and had made arrangements for someone to bartend while she was gone. It was good to have reliable friends.

She drove the 70 miles south to see her Dad and got there just in time to have breakfast. He was his same old self, reading the daily paper from one end to the other before he'd put it down. He always said that a newspaper was nothing more than the opinions of a lot of different people so most likely they were wrong about a lot of things. He always saved the crossword puzzle to do with his lunch.

Financially her father was in pretty good condition. He and his wife had lived modestly all their lives and saved a great deal of money. He always drove a new car and that was about his only vice in life.

"What sounds good to you for breakfast Maggie? That gal I married is a darned good cook."

"What I want for breakfast, I'm sure you don't have, so I'll settle for cakes and eggs."

"Tell me Maggie. What would you really like to have?" asked her Dad.

"Side pork, heavily peppered and crispy fried eggs and American fries. There's enough fat in that to kill a whole bunch of people."

They all laughed.

"Did you hear that Molly?" he yelled.

"Sure did."

She came around the corner with the coffee pot.

"I think that your Dad bought some fresh side pork yesterday, right after you called."

"Oh that sounds so good. I haven't had that in a long time."

They ate a big breakfast and then as the dishes were all cleared her dad asked her to come into the den for a minute.

"Maggie, you look like you're about to explode. Now let it out." and he reached back and shut the door lightly.

"Dad, Sarge has been arrested for murder. He's in jail in Wolf Creek, Alaska."

"Did he do it?"

"Well, yes and no. He shot and killed the man, but it wasn't murder. It was self defense."

"I haven't been in a courtroom for quite a while Maggie. The last law I practiced was about things like copyrights and legal contracts. It's been a pile of years since I was involved in a murder trial."

"Well Dad, I do know that the man who represents himself in court has a fool for a client. He really needs a good attorney and he needs him right away."

"Well said young lady. He most assuredly will need an attorney or he won't stand the chance of a snowball in hell. Any two bit prosecutor just out of law school could get him a lengthy sentence just on technicalities."

Together they talked for quite a while, Maggie relating all she knew about the case. They didn't seem to have much more to say, so together they went back out to the kitchen and poured another cup of coffee.

"Ever been to Alaska Molly?" asked Mr. Moore.


Maggie drove back up to the bar and when she came inside, she found a whole herd of bikers there. They all wished her and Sarge the best and wanted to help pay for an attorney. They were a damned rowdy bunch, but each and every one of them had a heart as big as Alaska. Sarge and Maggie were their friends and they weren't going to let Sarge go down without a good hard fight.

That evening at the appointed time, Sarge called.

"Anything new Maggie?"

"The only thing new is that Dad is going to represent you and he'll be there in just a couple days. Molly and I are coming too."

The phone was silent for a bit.

"Sarge? Are you there?"

"Yup."

"Things will be OK Sarge. Dad is one heck of an attorney."

"I sure didn't expect this Maggie. Your Dad is sure a fine person."

"Well Sarge, that's not entirely the whole story. He figured that once I finally found someone that would marry me, he doesn't want them getting away that easy."

Sarge had a big grin on his face.

"Love you Maggie."

"Love you too Sarge."

Plans were made and airline reservations were confirmed. The closest that they could fly was over a hundred miles away so they ended up hiring a bush pilot to take them the rest of the way in.

After some discussion on prices, destination and load, they walked over to an old yellow single engine plane that had certainly seen better days. They settled in and put on the safety belts. The pilot was walking around the plane, but it didn't look much like any kind of a pre-flight inspection. It was more like he was trying to find how to get in. If the wheels and wings were still there, it would probably fly for a while yet.

He got in and slammed the door behind him hard enough to shake the whole plane. He turned a switch and the prop spun; then it coughed and belched a cloud of black soot. After a short warmup the engine smoothed out some and they taxied out to the end of the runway. With a lot of noise and a big grin the pilot aimed it down the runway, gathering speed. Then the plane left the ground, banked hard left and headed upwards between two peaks.

Molly finally got up the courage to open her eyes and found that the whole place was beautiful. When she saw the earth going by between her feet though, she started to get a little scared. Some of those old planes had been in the air for a long time with darned little spent on them in the way of maintenance.

The trip to Wolf Creek was nothing less than spectacular. The plane was an old Dehaviland Beaver and it could carry a large payload, but only if asked nicely. The pilot appeared to be of the same vintage. It looked as if there was enough oil in his grubby old baseball cap to do an oil change.

Mountains towered off each wing of the small plane giving a view few had seen. Sometimes the pilot would bring the plane close to the edge of a cliff and then in a flash, the ground would fall away below showing another magnificent view. It gave them all a feeling of being very small.

The pilot smiled and pointed off to the right. On a ridge just a short distance away was a group of six Dall Sheep. They sparkled white in the sunshine, not bothering to run away.

The color was starting to leave Molly's face as was the usual smile. Small planes did quite a bit of rocking and rolling and her stomach was in near revolt. For her the flight seemed to go on forever.

They came down a few hundred feet and went right into a bank of fog so thick that nobody could see. The pilot squinted at his turn and bank indicator, altimeter, and then to his compass. He set the flaps and throttled back a bit, fine tuning the small crafts performance. He leveled the wings for a short way and then came out of the fog with the airstrip exactly where he thought it would be. The plane banked hard and lined up for final approach to the little grass strip they called an airport. With each sharp drop in altitude, Maggie could feel her stomach lurch.

A bounce and a bump, and they were rolling to a stop near the only hangar. The short flight was absolutely beautiful and the mountains were just as beautiful as the sky. The whole place was as if an artist had painted it.

They unloaded their belongings and turned to wave to their pilot. He was already back in the plane. The engine came to life once again and they watched as he lifted off, headed back home through the mountains. It didn't seem much different than hailing a cab in New York City.

They walked the three blocks to the town center and looked around. There wasn't much to the place but there was a hotel there and it looked to be in pretty good repair. None of them had packed much for baggage and figured to buy what they needed once they got there. There were still three weeks until trial and if all went well, that might just be enough time to mount a good defense.

The lady at the check-in desk asked what they would need for rooms and still being honeymooners, the attorney decided that they'd need two rooms. It wasn't a problem though since they were the only guests. It must have been the slow season.

The hotel served meals all day long so that was taken care of. All that was left was to find the Sheriff's Office.

Molly decided to take a nap so the attorney and his daughter walked the half block to see Sarge. They were quite surprised to see him sitting at the desk watching the television. He nearly had a heart attack when he saw Maggie.

"Maggie! When did you get here?"

She ran to him and gave him a big kiss.

"We just got here."

The attorney reached out his hand and Sarge went right past it to give him a big hug. He was after all, nearly family.

"Sure good to see you both. I don't know if I'd do too well without you."

They spent quite a bit of time talking, but it wasn't the usual family stuff. The attorney wanted to know everything and that meant everything he knew, including the gold and the killing. He wanted to know about Charlie and his drug habit and all about Sarge and his drug problem as well. By the time he got done, it was nearly 11:00 p.m. and time to call it a day. Just as they were about to leave, the Sheriff walked in and introduced himself. He stood about six feet tall and was nearly as wide across the shoulders.

"How in the hell can you let the prisoners walk around like this?" he asked the Sheriff laughing.

"Look around. Where in the hell could a man go? If he took off on a dead run, I could catch him before breakfast. It's wide open and nowhere to hide."

They all laughed.

"Besides, I just happen to think Sarge is a pretty honest man."

"We do too Sheriff. Can I come and talk to you tomorrow? I have a lot of questions."

"Sure. Unless we have a mass murder over night." and they all laughed.

"Bye Maggie." said Sarge.

That night he slept like a baby. The cavalry had arrived.

At 7:00 the attorney, Myron Moore arrived in the Sheriff's office. He was dressed in blue jeans and a sweatshirt, not exactly what the run of the mill attorney wears to work.

"Good morning Sheriff and you too Sarge. Got time for a few questions?"

They spent an hour going over things important to the case. One big item was where the body was found and who did the autopsy. When they had finished, the Sheriff agreed to take Mr. Moore to the spot that Charlie was found.

The Sheriff always used a four wheel drive vehicle just because of the nature of his work and the remoteness of the area. They got in and started to drive. Eventually they had to leave the dirt road and make their way across what looked like tundra. Several times, he nearly got stuck, but he seemed to know what he was doing.

After nearly three hours, they came to the river, the place they went over the falls.

"Here it is Mr. Moore. His body was hanging from this

branch, nearly three feet above the water line, still wrapped in the canvas. Funny that the animals hadn't eaten him."

Mr. Moore shot several photographs of the area.

"What condition was the body in?" he asked.

"Well, from the autopsy report, it had several broken bones, but that was most surely done after he was killed. It would account for what Sarge said about going over the falls."

Mr. Moore looked the Sheriff straight in the, eye trying to gauge his reaction.

"What was the cause of death according to the coroners report?"

"I thought you already knew that!"

"I might have heard, but tell me again Sheriff."

"Suffocation and gunshot, but most probably suffocation."

"What the hell do you mean suffocation?"

They were standing near the river and the noise of the water made it hard to hear.

"He was shot in the abdomen but it didn't hit anything vital except his middle spine. Then he was wrapped in a canvas and that's how he died. Suffocation." said the Sheriff.

"Damn."

"He might have died later from the gunshot, but the coroner said that it was the lack of air inside the canvas that killed him."

"The gunshot to the spine and being wrapped in the canvas would have made it impossible for him to move wouldn't it?"

"That's right." said the Sheriff.

"So what are the grounds for a charge of murder?"

"When Sarge wrapped him in the canvas, he was still alive. He might have survived if it were just the gunshot, but it looks like he really wanted the man dead and suffocated him to finish the job."

The attorney pursed his lips and looked around for a bit.

"Can we drive anywhere close to the top of the falls?" asked Mr. Moore.

"I think we can, but it might take a while to get there."

"If you don't mind too much, I sure would like to see what Sarge saw just before he went over the edge."

"Sure."

They drove around some pretty rocky areas and only had to walk a couple blocks to get a view. As they stood looking, the first thing that came to Mr. Moore was that any damned fool could have kept himself from going over that falls.

"This place doesn't look so bad." said Mr. Moore.

"You gotta remember that it was in the late fall and the river was way up when all of this happened."

"Do you think that drugs were involved?" he asked the Sheriff.

"No. That's one thing they didn't find any trace of. The man was as clean as a new born baby. If he was a user, it had to be a long time before."

"Ya know Sheriff, this thing may have played out just the way Sarge said it did. He may have shot the man in self defense and wrapped him in the canvas to transport the body down river."

They both sat on a log, going back and forth over the whole incident. Mr. Moore was pretty sure Sarge had given him the whole story.

"I suppose it's possible, but the new prosecutor is out to make a name for himself and Sarge might just wind up being his first victim."

"Don't be too sure." said the attorney. Deep inside, he was planning his case in great detail.

Their trip back to Wolf Creek took a bit longer than usual with the Sheriff taking the long way around, showing Mr. Moore some of the most beautiful country in the world. They came across a huge herd of caribou and saw a pack of wolves following closely. They were intent on looking for a weak or injured animal, something that would make a good meal.

The next day, Mr. Moore went before the Judge asking that the bail be dropped to $100,000 if the accused agreed to stay in the town of Wolf Creek and be in by 10:00 each night. The Judge thought about it for a while and then asked the Sheriff what he thought about the idea. So with the approval of all concerned except for the prosecutor, Sarge was a free man, almost. Mr. Moore put up the bail money for him and that meant that he was free to spend some time with Maggie.

Their first night alone darned near killed poor old Sarge. Maggie had saved all her energy for him and it seemed that she couldn't get enough. They would no more than finish a nice warm shower than she was ready to go again. They made love the way Maggie liked it, hard and with no rest for the wicked. Sarge too had saved a lot for his woman so between them, the nails in the floorboards were loosened some. Nothing though that a good carpenter couldn't fix.

"You seem to be slowing up Maggie. What's the problem anyway?" he chided her.

"You're the one who cried uncle first."

He took her hand and pulled her down to him. They kissed long and deeply, snuggling close under the warm blankets. Within very few minutes they both came alive once more, going for number three in just a couple hours. They had indeed missed each other badly.

With the trial looming just a short time away, it was time for Mr. Moore to get busy with his defense tactics. He had met the prosecutor and like he figured, the man was barely out of law school. The jurors would be picked from the community and that in itself might be a problem. There were few murders in this little town and public sentiment might just be against the "baby killer". The Viet Nam war was still going on and the newspapers were having a field day, making the military look like murderers.

Mr. Moore made an appointment with the prosecutor, trying to get a feel for his methods. He wasn't treated too kindly and was politely told that anything concerning the upcoming trial will only be handled with written correspondence. Then he was shown the door.

The hackles had been raised on the Federal Attorney's neck

and it looked like it was going to be a real fight. Back in the lower 48, there were expert witnesses that would testify to anything you were willing to pay for. He had some markers out and had every intention of calling them all in. There were trial attorneys that would eat a prosecutor like this for a snack and a lot of them owed their existence to Mr. Moore.

That evening, he called a few close friends in Washington and had their promise that they'd be in Wolf Creek the following Monday morning, bright and early, even if they had to swim to get there. One of their greatest problems was that of having the body back in Minnesota. They needed to have it exhumed and another forensic study done on it. This was going to all be handled by Dr. James Madison, another attorney he'd helped along the way. He was a forensic pathologist and a damned good lawyer to boot. He had won some very high profile cases in his career.

Next he'd need at least a half dozen expert witnesses concerning gunshot and suffocation cases. This was going to be a tough one because of the rarity of this happening. If he died of suffocation, it would throw a whole new light on the case.

There was the matter of Sarge's service record and his medical records. He was pretty sure that he'd been honest with him, but during the trial was no time for surprises. He also wanted any financial information there might be about him.

Finally he wanted someone that had dealt with animal attacks, more specifically bear attacks on humans and that might be hard to get. The Chief Administrator of the U.S.

Forest Service had been his roommate a long time ago and he might just remember him. All in all, things were shaping up.

Dinner time came and the four from Minnesota sat together at a quiet table in the hotel's dining room. The food was excellent and Maggie was dressed fit to kill. Her new step-mother too was dressed beautifully. The food was good and a bottle of wine was a nice compliment to their evenings fine dining.

"Sarge, we need to talk and I think tomorrow will work well for me. Then on Monday morning, we have a staff of professionals coming in. We'll have to do it all over again just in case we might miss something."

"What do you mean 'a staff of professionals'?" asked Sarge.

"Well Son, I had a few friends over the years that owe me a couple favors. Now it's time to collect. They will all be here by Monday morning."

"See Sarge? Dad will do all he can and here's one not many know. He never lost a court case in his entire career." said Maggie.

"He loses one once in a while at home though." said Molly laughing.

"One thing I have learned over the years is that you take nothing for granted and prepare twice as well as you think you'll need to." said Mr. Moore.

Saturday came and Sarge went over to check in with the Sheriff. He didn't want anyone thinking he'd left the country.

From there it was off to see his attorney. Mr. Moore was

sitting at the little desk making notes on a yellow legal pad. He seemed to be a bit lost in his thoughts.

"Are you ready Mr. Moore?" asked Sarge.

"In just a few minutes. I'm taking some last minute notes on things I want to ask you."

"Hi Molly. Did you get a good nights sleep?"

"Sure did Sarge. We leave the windows open all night and pile on the blankets." she laughed.

After a short bit of conversation, Mr. Moore stood up and walked toward the door.

"I rented the next door room so we'll have some privacy." said the attorney.

He unlocked the door and entered, motioning for Sarge to sit down at the table. The bed had been removed and there were at least 20 chairs and 5 small tables. It looked an awful lot like an office. There were phones on each table as well.

Mr. Moore turned on a recorder and moved a microphone close to Sarge. Then he asked him to speak so he could test the recording levels. Everything seemed to be in good order.

"Tell me your full name and date of birth please."

It had the feeling of being in a courtroom with Perry Mason.

The day passed and they finished up at nearly 3:00.

"How ya feeling now that you've opened your entire past to a stranger?"

"Well, first off, you're no stranger." and they laughed.

"Actually, you've had a pretty normal life with a few exceptions. There doesn't seem to be anything there that the prosecution could use. That business of shooting the child in Viet Nam was a bad one, but it was war after all."

"That's the way that I see it, but it might be thought of as being part of a pattern." said Sarge.

"Usually it takes three events to indicate a trend, but a good attorney could insinuate a trend, like having a short fuse."

Downstairs in the hotel, there was a pool table and Mr. Moore was pretty darned good at eight ball. He beat Sarge nearly every time they played. Saturday night he was about to break. He chalked up the cue and started to shoot. He pulled back and just as he went to move the stick forward, someone bumped him from behind and the cue ball went into the corner pocket. He turned to see who had the nerve to ruin his shot.

"Jim! Well for gosh sake it's been a lot of years." said Mr. Moore shaking hands with him.

"It sure has Myron. I understand you need some help."

Dr. James Madison had arrived in the town of Wolf Creek, Alaska.

"Tomorrow there is a bunch more coming too, but they had a hard time getting here. Not many planes available, but they said to tell you that they'd be here tomorrow, and you can count on that."

## Chapter: 14    Meeting of the Minds

By Sunday afternoon the entire group of requested professionals had arrived and with them came one extra, Martin Smith, Private Detective. The only one that knew his occupation was Mr. Moore and he had requested the man personally. He would dig around and if there was a skunk in the woodpile, he'd expose him.

On Monday, they all met in the hotel room that was made into an office. There were seven days until the trial would begin. There were legal maneuvers that could delay the trial, but the whole team figured that it was time to get on with it.

"What did you come up with when you exhumed the body?" asked Mr. Moore.

"Well," said Dr. Madison, "the body was in pretty bad condition. Forensic studies showed that the victim died of a gunshot wound and that was the end of it. The angle of the gunshot was consistent with what the accused stated. The victim was standing within a distance of 5-10 feet away. There were gun powder burns on his lower torso. Part of the bullet was still wedged into his spine."

"So what is your opinion Jim?"

"The victim died within a couple minutes of a gunshot wound."

"No suffocation?"

"None. The bullet hit the liver and exploded it. And furthermore Myron, I want to talk with the man who came to that conclusion. Do you think that I should subpoena him for the trial?"

"Probably a good idea Jim. Thanks."

"Next we need to know about the serology report." said Mr. Moore.

Another doctor stood up.

"As far as we can tell Myron, he was an unusually large man and had used cocaine within two hours of his death. The lining inside his nose was eroded as if he had been a habitual and long time user. From a medical standpoint, he rarely missed a day. His nasal turbinates were completely wiped out."

"Are you positive?" asked Myron.

"Positive."

"Thanks."

They went from person to person around the room and when they had all finished, it didn't look at all like it did before the meeting. In fact, there was a great possibility that a lot of what had been said of Sarge was manufactured. Actually to be more specific, it was all a ball of lies, an effort to get an easy conviction for the inept prosecutor.

"Thank you all for your efforts. Trial is a week from now and I want us all to meet once more on Friday night right here in this same place. I want you all to work like you haven't in years. I smell a rat." said Myron Moore.

With that, they all went different directions. Mr. Moore sat alone in the room for quite a while trying to envision what the trial would go like. Prosecution would have their best shot and then he would get his chance.

There was a knock on the door.

"Come in. It's open."

"Thanks." he said and walked in.

"Oh. Hi Martin. Thanks for stopping by."

"Glad to Myron. I think I might just owe you a favor or two."

Mr. Moore waved his hand as if to dismiss his comment.

"I think there's a rat loose in Wolf Creek and I want you to find him. Start with the prosecutor and let me know what you come up with. Meet me here tomorrow night about the same time. Any questions?" He sat at the desk tapping his fingers on the telephone.

"None."

The door shut and he was gone as fast as he'd arrived. This was an all business detective and when he got on a trail, he was like a bloodhound. His career in New York had taken him to some very high profile cases and his penchant for murder gave him a lot of experience. He too was a family man, but there was never any mention of it. Job and family did not mix for him.

Maggie and Sarge had been staying pretty close to their room and the restaurant. Myron didn't want him to go anywhere until the trial was over. When he was in public, there had to be others around. Molly was getting a bit bored with the whole thing, but stayed close to Maggie at all times. There wasn't much in the way of places to go shopping, but off the main street, she found a place to buy native artwork. She bought enough to supply an entire art gallery.

The time arrived for the detective's report and Myron went over to their office.

"Well, it looks like our boy is in need of a win at any cost. He passed his bar exam but nobody knows how since he was hardly ever at class. Then his 'Daddy' got him this job. He's a legislator in Fairbanks. So far he hasn't been to trial once. All cases are settled out of court."

"How long has he been here?" asked Myron.

"It's just over a year and a half now. There were some cases where men were arrested for drugs and they settled by paying a small fine. Looks like he's taking kickbacks. There's a lot of locals that he's in bed with and it's going to be tough to get an untainted jury."

"Thanks for all your help Martin. Can you stick around until after the trial?"

"Anything for an old friend."

"Good. Good."

The week was moving along at a rapid pace with the entire

team working hard to prepare the case. Myron had an adviser that would sit at the defense table with him. He was a high dollar lawyer and he looked at the case as being almost a vacation.

The final meeting of the minds brought little new information, but it did appear that the prosecutor was a gambler too, a nice habit if you can afford it.

The jury had been selected earlier in the week from a pool of 18 men and women. Myron used up his challenges and was forced to accept a couple men that he knew were a little less than good jurors. The prosecutor fought hard for those two which made Myron suspicious of his motives. He had Martin Smith check on them, looking for anything that might shed light on their apparent value to the prosecution.

On Sunday night Martin Smith arrived with the information he had asked for. They went into the office.

"What have you found on those two jurors Martin?"

"Well Myron, the first one has a brother that is going to stand trial for selling drugs, but nobody knows when. He was arrested over a year ago and it seems that the prosecutor is just using him at will. Any time he needs something, he threatens to take it to trial. Kind of like having him on a leash."

"What about the other one. He looks like a nice enough guy."

"That's a whole different story. His name is Art Whitebird. He's 32 years old and has a family of two kids and a nice wife. He runs a bulldozer for a road gang. His mother was arrested for welfare fraud by the local authorities. Here's another case that's over a year old and hasn't come to trial. He's sitting on it, just like the other one. What bothers me most is the possibility that there might be others. The prosecutor needs a win on this one and he's pulled out all the stops." said Martin.

"Thanks. You've done a good job for me but I need you to keep digging. Look at the prosecutor's gambling habits and the possibility of a girlfriend."

"I'll do that."

Martin Smith had a most determined look on his face.

It was near 1:00 p.m. and Myron took out his little black book of phone numbers. He punched the buttons slowly and deliberately.

"This is Myron Moore. Is the Judge in please?"

He waited for just a few moments and the Judge came on the line.

"Myron. How the hell are ya?"

"Just fine Judge. I got a real problem here. We got a dirty prosecutor in a murder trial and it looks like I'll be needing some help. Can you get up to Wolf Creek, Alaska by Monday morning?"

"I'll be there. I'll have to re-schedule some cases but that shouldn't be any trouble. Don't tell anyone at all who I am though. I'll bring my legal aide and say that it's my daughter. We'll take separate rooms. I owe you one Myron, but just by chance is the fishing any good there?"

Sunday night all the requested help was in place. The Judge

had arrived and all of the others were ready. The last minute meeting yielded nothing new.

"Now this is important. I want you all in the courtroom and I want you where I can see you. If something very important comes to mind, I want you to cough twice. Not loudly mind you, but loud enough to get my attention. Then I'll ask for a short recess. Are there any questions?" asked Mr. Moore.

He looked around the room for responses.

"Thank you all. Get a good nights rest. See you in court at 10:00."

Everyone left the room, making no unnecessary noise. This was an extremely professional gathering of legal minds.

That evening Sarge and Maggie dined together with her family. Nothing was said about the trial and talk was kept to things like fishing and gardening, trying to keep things upbeat for them all. Sarge kept thinking that this might just be his last meal with them all and it saddened him some.

There was a small lull in the conversation.

"Thanks to you all for the support you've given me." said Sarge.

"Now, now, now. Lets not get sentimental. Do you know much about the fishing in this part of the world?" asked Myron. He was doing his level best to keep the talk away from the courtroom.

That night as Sarge lay next to Maggie, his thoughts turned back once more to the drugs that got him into this predicament. He had come a long way from Viet Nam to Alaska with some real bad side trips. His addiction to heroine felt as strong as it had ever been. He rolled onto his side and put his arm over Maggie. He thought of the day he first met her in that ward in Viet Nam. He thought of how she told him her name, "Herman". From somewhere deep inside, he heard that same old song once more, "You must remember this, a kiss is still a kiss, a sigh is just a sigh. The fundamental things apply, as time goes by."

Tears welled in his eyes once more. He had to get through this trial and all that went with it. He knew inside that there would be some damned tough questions asked, but he wasn't sure that he'd be able to answer them. He felt as if he were floating off into space and the only thing that kept him here was Maggie, his security, his stability. He blinked the tears away and fell into a sound sleep.

In Anchorage, Martin Smith had just lost $500.00 to a small time hustler from Wolf Creek. It was the prosecutor and he was a regular at a gambling spot in the basement of a large hotel. The high rollers gathered here on the weekends and were treated well hoping they'd leave behind a ton of cash. Women of all colors, sizes and shapes did their best to make the gamblers feel like big spenders.

The prosecutor loved to play poker and had a blonde on each arm as he played. It was worth it to see how he thought he was such a big spender. One good looking redhead found her way to Martin Smith's shoulder.

"How ya like getting the hell kicked out of ya by a small

time hustler?" she asked.

"Not too well babe. Got any suggestions?"

"He'll be playing high stakes poker in a while in a private room. Ya want in?"

"How high?"

"No limit." she said.

"Now that's my kind of game."

"I can get ya in, but ya better stick with me. And another thing, I don't come cheap. Five bills will get you in and I'll throw in a back rub later."

"Deal." and he peeled off the required amount.

She appeared to be the kind of woman that made her wants and wishes known, the kind that could wear you out, hurt you and make you come back for more.

They played the slot machines for a while until the appointed time.

"These damned machines don't ever pay off." said Martin.

"No. These slot machines are what build the big casinos in Vegas."

"Not with my money." and he pressed the payout button, putting the change in his pocket.

"Ready for some action?"

"I'd like to, but I really want to get my money back right now."

"Not that kind of action lover boy." she said.

"Oh. I guess I'm ready." he said with a grin.

The room was about as well decorated as the Taj Mahal.

They had spared no expense to make this a den for just the big boys. The place had brought in its own supply of women too, but it was plain to see that they were working for the house. Not at all like the redhead on Martin's arm. She sat behind him and to the left, being quiet, watching.

The play started with an ante of $500 which made the detective inhale a little deeply.

"Too much for you?" asked the prosecutor.

"No. I just got a whiff of Red's perfume."

A couple of them laughed. The cards were dealt and Martin looked to see what he had, but tried hard to look nonchalant. Ace of spades, ace of hearts, king of spades, king of diamonds and a deuce of hearts. Two pair, just enough to get yourself killed.

The first man out opened for a thousand and that killed off the next man. The rest called until it came to the big spender.

"I'll raise that another five grand." and he smiled around the table.

Now it was down to four players. The whole table was a bit tense at how fast the stakes had gone through the ceiling.

"Cards gentlemen?" asked the dealer.

The big man took two, meaning he already had three of a kind. Each man stuck it out and hoped for a good draw. Martin broke up his two pair and drew three.

"Opener's bet." said the dealer.

"I'll bet a thousand." said the opener.

"I'll raise that another $5,000." said the prosecutor and

threw five big chips out to the middle of the green velvet.

"I'll raise that another ten said the next man." throwing in the appropriate amount of chips.

The next man called hoping he could afford to stay in.

Then it was Martin's turn. He looked again and found that he'd drawn another ace giving him three Aces. He called.

The big prosecutor seemed to be thinking about how much money he had. Then he called the banker over and whispered in his ear. He nodded his head and the game went on. He made the pot right and then raised another twenty thousand. That was way too rich for Martin so he bailed out as did the man next to him. Even with three aces, he just didn't have that much money with him. The game played out with the big man investing over 50 thousand in the first hand.

It was show and tell time. The player across the table turned over a full house, queens over threes. The big man turned livid and threw his cards face down on the table.

"Bastard. You haven't seen the last of me." said the attorney.

He got up and walked out of the room slamming the door as he left. Martin followed him at a distance being lead to the airport, and saw him get into a small twin engine Beech. It was getting near daylight and the plane lifted off and headed to the southeast. There was still time to get that back-rub and report to Myron before court. Martin followed an hour later, getting in at almost 9 a.m.

"He's into them in a big way. I saw him drop 50 grand in one hand." he told the attorney.

"Thanks Martin."

## Chapter: 15    Trial

"All rise." said the bailiff. "The Honorable Judge Wendell Anderson presiding."

"Be seated."

He was a gruff sounding man in his mid sixties with snow white hair. He ruffled through his stack of papers and picked one out.

"The case before us today is a charge of murder in the first degree. William Stone, you are charged with the murder of Charles Wilson, a black man from Minneapolis Minnesota. You William Stone, have plead not guilty at an earlier hearing."

He looked over at Sarge and spoke again.

"Are you represented by counsel?"

"Yes Your Honor. Mr. Myron Moore."

The Judge looked over at Mr. Moore.

"I think I've read some of your legal briefs before. It's good to see you in my court. Prosecutor, have you witnesses that you wish to call?"

"I do Your Honor."

"Then get on with it.'

The prosecutor went through several witnesses, people that found the body, others that had been there. Myron thought that it was particularly interesting that he didn't call the doctor who did the autopsy.

He started reading the statements that Sarge had made when he was first charged with the crime. After that came the reading of his service record.

"It seems that you have a taste for killing Mr. Stone." said the prosecutor.

Nearly the entire courtroom coughed twice and at the very same time.

"Objection." said Myron.

"Sustained." said the Judge.

After a couple hours, the prosecution rested its case and then it was Myron's turn.

"Your Honor, I'd like to call as my first witness, the doctor who did the original autopsy, Dr. Samuel Grossman."

The Judge looked around the courtroom and didn't see him.

"It appears as if the good Doctor didn't make it." said the Judge.

The bailiff walked up to the bench and whispered to the Judge.

"Thank you. Ahh Mr. Moore. It appears as if the good doctor won't be coming. He drowned while fishing yesterday."

He leaned over and whispered to Sarge.

"How damned convenient."

The federal Judge Henry Lawson was sitting in the back of the courtroom taking notes. His legal aide was writing as fast as she could. The remainder of the team was taking notes as well. It seemed to be a stroke of providence for the prosecution, that the doctor would perish at the appropriate time.

"Please call Dr. James Madison." said Myron.

The doctor was sworn in and sat down. After a few questions about his credentials, Myron went to work, meticulous and tenacious.

"And did the victim suffer long after the gunshot?"

"No. He died within a very short time."

"Was there any evidence that he was suffocated."

"None whatsoever."

"Here is a copy of the autopsy report done by the recently deceased doctor. Have you seen this before?"

"Yes I have."

"And from what you have seen during the autopsy, does it compare well to what you have read in Dr. Grossman's report?" asked Myron.

Dr. Madison turned to look at the Judge.

"Please answer the question." asked the Judge.

"The autopsy report I have read concerning the death of Charles Wilson, was evidently done by a man who either had not seen the body or was totally incompetent. The cause of death was gunshot wound, not suffocation, and the autopsy that I personally did is consistent with what Mr. Stone has said in his statements to the Sheriff. The victim was standing 5-10 feet from Mr. Stone when he shot Charles Wilson. The bullet was from a .357 magnum and totally destroyed the victim's liver causing immediate death."

"Thank you." said Mr. Moore. "Your witness Mr. Prosecutor."

"No questions."

Here was a golden opportunity for the prosecution to make the new autopsy report look bad because of the passage of time. He chose not to take the opportunity. Myron was a bit confused, and asked for a short recess.

The team walked out into the hallway.

"What in the world is going on in there? Is he inept or is he so confident of the verdict that he doesn't need to be concerned?"

Altogether they figured that he had the jury in his pocket. He would get the verdict that he asked for.

"Do you all agree that we should continue with testimony?"

They all agreed and went back into the courtroom.

"Your Honor, I'd like to call the Chief Administrator of the U.S. Forest Service."

He was sworn in and took a seat in the witness box.

"Do you have any expertise in bear attacks?"

"Yes sir. I investigate all attacks within the boundaries of the Forest Service."

"Have you had the opportunity to review the two autopsy reports?"

"Yes I have."

"And do you see any inconsistencies between them?"

"Yes I do. The first autopsy report had no mention of the bear bite on the back of the victims head. There was a fracture of the skull behind both ears, as if he had been bitten in the head by a large bear. The first autopsy made no mention of this."

"And is that a common type of wound in bear attacks?"

"It is to some degree, less damage than usual. It was as if the man didn't fight back, like he just fell down and stayed there, not provoking the animal. That is what usually gets a person killed, fighting back."

"Thank you. Your witness Mr. Prosecutor." said Myron.

"No questions."

Again the entire courtroom was surprised.

Mr. Moore called another doctor who specialized in serology. He told of his findings of recent cocaine use and the condition of his nose. When he was finished, he offered the witness to the prosecutor with the same result.

The proceedings had progressed at a rather rapid rate and by 2:00 p.m. they were nearly finished with the witness list. They all went to the hotel for something to eat.

"Now Sarge we have a hard one for you. If I call you as a witness, you can tell the jury how everything played out. The danger is that the prosecution has a chance then to question you. That might be a tough one."

He thought for a time and nodded his head.

"I do want to testify."

"No Sarge." said Maggie. "They'll really make you look bad."

"I want you all to know this. I am not a bad man. I killed in self defense, and under the same circumstances, I'd probably do it again."

"The only thing I can do then is to be thorough before he gets his chance at you. I'm going to ask you all the hard questions first."

Back in the courtroom, the Judge had returned and sat down, calling for order.

"Mr. Moore, do you have any further witnesses?"

"Yes Your Honor. One final witness. I call the accused, Mr. William Stone."

He walked up to the stand and was sworn in. The questioning covered everything from his childhood to the present. He asked about his parents and his ex-wife. Then he went to his service record going over all of his decorations.

"And did you ever kill any unarmed civilians?" asked Myron.

"I did once when a young kid came at me with what I thought was a grenade. A friend of mine had just been killed in the same manner and I was nervous. After I shot and killed him, I found out that he only had a candy bar in his hand, and not a grenade."

The courtroom was unusually quiet.

"And did you ever use illegal drugs?"

"Yes I did. When I was in the hospital, I needed it for pain and before I knew it, I was and still am, an addict. I fight it every day."

"And when was the last time you used drugs?"

"Several months ago. Almost a year."

They went through everything with his father and how his wife had left him several times for another man.

"And why didn't you divorce her?" asked Myron.

"I loved her."

Again the courtroom was quiet. The questioning covered nearly everything in his entire life. Myron was doing his utmost to make Sarge look very human, like a kind and considerate man.

"I have no further questions Your Honor."

"Mr. Prosecutor, do you have any questions today?" asked the Judge.

"No Your Honor."

"This is most unusual." said the Judge. "I'll hear closing arguments tomorrow at 10:00 a.m. The jury will not speak of the case to each other or anyone else."

And with that, the Judge banged the gavel. Everyone stood and he left the room.

That evening, they all dined in the office for privacy and a chance to discuss strategy.

"It would seem that all of our preparations were for nothing. He has not even shown a good case for murder. There isn't a jury in the world that would convict Sarge in this case." said

Myron.

"I wouldn't think so either, but stranger things have happened." said Molly.

After they finished their meal, Myron stood and addressed the gathering.

"I think that we've just seen a case where there was no case. The prosecution is inept and from what I've seen, he shouldn't be practicing law."

They all agreed, and within a few minutes had retired for the night, leaving just Myron in the room.

Again there was a knock on the door.

"Come."

Martin Smith walked in and gave his report.

"That prosecutor is in debt up to his eyeballs. He has two girlfriends and a kid by the first one. He deals in drugs but just small time, and gambles to excess. If he gets a win in this case, his father has promised to bail him out. That's a lot of incentive to be a crook."

"Sure looks that way." said Myron.

That evening, Sarge stepped out onto the balcony of their room and closed the door behind him. A lot of time had passed from when he was first able to remember. He thought of his Mother and if he squeezed his eyes real tight, he could still see her face. He could remember her holding him close when he fell from the swing. He thought of how she cooked his favorite meals when his Father wasn't there. And he remembered the day she left, the last day he ever saw her again. His Father had been yelling loudly at her and when he awoke in the morning, there was nobody there to cook breakfast for him. He remembered that there was a time his Father only sobered up when he ran out of money for whiskey. There just had to be some good memories inside his head, there just had to be. He thought that he might have had a sister too, but he wasn't sure.

Clouds of bad memories covered him like smoke from a fire. There seemed to be little good in his life until he met Maggie. He felt a little old for having kids, but if Maggie ever wanted to start a family, he'd do whatever it took to be a good Dad.

The whole thing was now coming to a close and he figured that he might not like the way the story ended. He was scared alright, but his biggest fear wasn't doing time in a prison, it was losing Maggie. She had been his lifeline, his friend, his lover, and life just wouldn't be worth much without her next to him.

The very tops of the mountains were covered with thin wispy clouds and as the sun set, they turned a brilliant red. He walked back inside and closed the door behind him. This might be his last time to spend with Maggie. He sat down on the bed and took his clothes off. Then he pulled back the blankets and snuggled close to her.

Closing arguments started at 10:00 a.m. and the prosecutor gave it his best shot, trying to make Sarge look like a baby killer gone crazy, while using drugs on a canoe trip. He made him look like a wanton murderer that found out he liked to kill when he was in Viet Nam. He painted the sergeant with a broad brush, trying to make the jury glad to put him away.

Myron took his turn.

"What you have here ladies and gentlemen is a case of self defense. Charles Wilson had been using drugs and while wandering around looking for gold, he ran into a bear that caught him and bit him. He got away and the bear followed trying to kill him. Charlie found a cave to hide in and Sarge saved him scaring the bear away with his revolver. Later that night Charlie went crazy, either from the drugs or the bear bite to his head, or maybe both. He hit sarge over the head trying to kill him. Then he came back in the dark once more trying to finish him off. This time Sarge was injured badly. The third time, Sarge was ready and when he came to finish him, he shot him once. Charlie lay close by and didn't move at all.

Sarge wrapped up his head wound and rolled Charlie up in a canvas. He put the corpse into the canoe and headed for the nearest authorities. Unfortunately he didn't make it. He was swept over the falls and lost nearly everything including Charlie's body. Finally after a couple days, Sarge was rescued by some hunters and made his way to the Sheriff's Office here in Wolf Creek. The rest is on the record.

Sarge is a good man, charged with a crime he didn't do. In your deliberations, take into account the fact that he was the one that sought out the authorities. He was the one that paddled for days to bring Charlie's body home to his wife. If he were a criminal, he'd have ditched the body somewhere saying that he had gotten lost. Ladies and gentlemen, this is an innocent man and you must find him not guilty."

With that, the jury retired to deliberate and the Judge recessed until the verdict came in. It might only take a couple hours or sometimes it could go on for days.

There was no verdict the first day and this had Myron a bit concerned. Then they waited all of the next day with no verdict. By the end of the third day, the jury asked the Judge for advice. The foreman said that they were deadlocked and the Judge was infuriated.

"You go back in and talk between yourselves. There will be no hung juries here in my court." said the Judge.

They took a break for lunch and when they came back, they came to a unanimous verdict rather quickly. Everyone was called back to court.

The Judge banged the gavel and all was silent.

"Mr. Foreman, have you come to a verdict?"

"We have you honor."

"Hand it to the bailiff. Thank you for all of your hard deliberations. You jurors are all dismissed."

They all stood and left the courtroom.

"Bailiff hand me the verdict." said the Judge.

He looked it over and handed it back to the bailiff.

"Bailiff, please read the decision."

"We the jury in the case of the death of Charles Wilson, find Mr. William Stone guilty of murder in the first degree."

"And was this a unanimous verdict?"

"It was Your Honor." said the bailiff.

"Mr. William Stone, please stand. You have been found guilty by a jury of your peers in the murder of Charles Wilson. Sentencing will be tomorrow at 3:00 p.m. Sheriff take the prisoner into custody. I mean real custody this time."

Sarge was handcuffed and lead out of the courtroom, leaving behind Maggie, crying hard and Molly trying her best to console her. Seated next to her was Myron. He was not a happy attorney.

He turned in his chair and looked back at his team. Then he looked over to the Federal Judge Henry Lawson, but he had already left the courtroom.

Myron walked over to Dr. Madison and told him to gather the group in the office at 8:00 that night. There were things that needed to be discussed. Then he looked over at the prosecutor. He had a big grin and was talking quite animatedly to a little man in a black suit, no doubt a friend of his father. This was the big win that would make him a new man.

The group gathered that evening and unanimously stated that it was a fixed jury. One or two held out for a guilty verdict until the rest weakened. These were the two that the detective Martin Smith had mentioned. It was plain to see what had happened.

Later that day, Maggie, Molly and Myron all went to see Sarge. He was locked in a cell and there wasn't a chance he'd get out any time soon. Sarge's face had changed. There used to be a set of smile creases at the corner of each eye, but they had left with the verdict. In his mind there was no longer anything to smile about.

"We'll appeal the verdict to a higher court Sarge." said Myron.

"The way you all talked, it was a sure thing I'd be found innocent. Now here I sit and the prospects for getting out look pretty bad."

"I don't want to give you any false hope Sarge. It does look bad right now. I remember an old saying from when I used to be a baseball fan. 'It ain't over 'til the fat lady sings'. Well, I haven't heard anyone singing yet."

And with that he walked outside leaving the rest visiting Sarge. He walked over to the hotel office and went inside. He had no more than gotten settled in his chair than there was a knock on the door. It was Judge Henry Lawson.

"Come in Judge. It's good to see you."

"You too Myron. It's been a lot of years."

"Have a chair."

"Thanks. Well, I have a feeling that you were right. There is a bad taste in my mouth and it's not going away. There's some shady dealings here and I have the authority to fix it. I don't think that the Judge is involved, but the prosecutor is in this one all the way."

"I agree Judge, but I'm not too sure of how to handle this. We could file for an appeal, but that might take years to get. William Stone is an innocent man and it really digs at me to see him sitting in a cell."

"I know what you mean Myron. This business of the law is

wide open for corruption if we don't watch each other. It seems to me that there is way too much power in one man's hand."

"I agree, but it is rare"

"I am going to call a grand jury for tomorrow at 1:00. My clerk is finishing the subpoenas right now."

"Who all is on the list."

"Each and every person who spoke in court. Each and every one." he mused.

At 8:00 a.m. there was a whole courtroom full of people, potential jurors. Subpoenas were passed out like sandwiches. Several of Myron's legal team were hired by Henry Lawson to help with the proceedings. The witness list read almost like the one from the previous trial.

At 1:00 the Grand Jury was called and the proceedings began with a statement by the Judge as to what the penalty was for perjury. Justice would be swift and sure for anyone that trifled with this court. There were even some federal Marshals there to get things done.

The Judge started to speak and the courtroom door opened wide and in came the prosecutor wearing a set of shiny stainless steel handcuffs. He was escorted by two U.S. Marshals.

"Now what is this about?" asked the Judge.

"He was trying to leave the area in a small bush plane Your Honor. He wouldn't come peaceably so we arrested him."

The Judge looked at the prosecutor.

"Now what was your name again?"

The prosecutor sat still through the proceedings watching his fancy lifestyle flee in front of him. There was talk about witness tampering, bribery, drugs, gambling, politics and the biggest of all jury tampering. By the time it was over, the big man was hanging his head and the Marshal's came and took the cuffs off Sarge for good.

Judge Wendell Anderson was cleared of any wrongdoing, but was transferred to a different court in another part of the state, much further north. The two jurors that were involved each got a one year sentence with work release privileges. The Sheriff is still there in Wolf Creek. There's not much work to do, but it gives him some time to fish.

Myron and Judge Lawson spent some much needed time fishing and renewed their friendship of years back. Myron was, after a few days, anxious to go back to reading his paper each morning even if he didn't believe it all.

Sarge was another case. He and Maggie took the first available plane to Minnesota and were home at Herman's Hangout by early the next day. The bikers seemed glad to see them.

Sarge and Maggie married on the river in the spot that they had picked. The whole community wished them well and business picked up quite a bit.

Now in the evenings when there aren't any customers, Sarge will go and get his maps, unrolling them on the top of the pool table. A single light bulb over that pool table is nearly all the